DANCE, SUGARPLUM

AURELIA KNIGHT AMY OLIVEIRA

Copyright © 2024 by Aurelia Knight and Amy Oliveira

All rights reserved.

No part of this book may be reproduced in any form or by any electronic or mechanical means, including information storage and retrieval systems, without written permission from the author, except for the use of brief quotations in a book review.

This is an ARC.

CONTENT WARNING

Dance, Sugarplum is a dark Christmas romance with triggering themes and content throughout. This is a nutcracker retelling.

This book contains graphic, violent, and sexual content that may be upsetting to some readers. The following lists some, not all, of the potentially sensitive subjects included. If you have a specific concern please reach out on Aurelia or Amy's socials.

Dub/non-con, abuse of power, light impact play, somnophilia, stalking, sexual advances from a family member, murder, gun violence, manipulation.

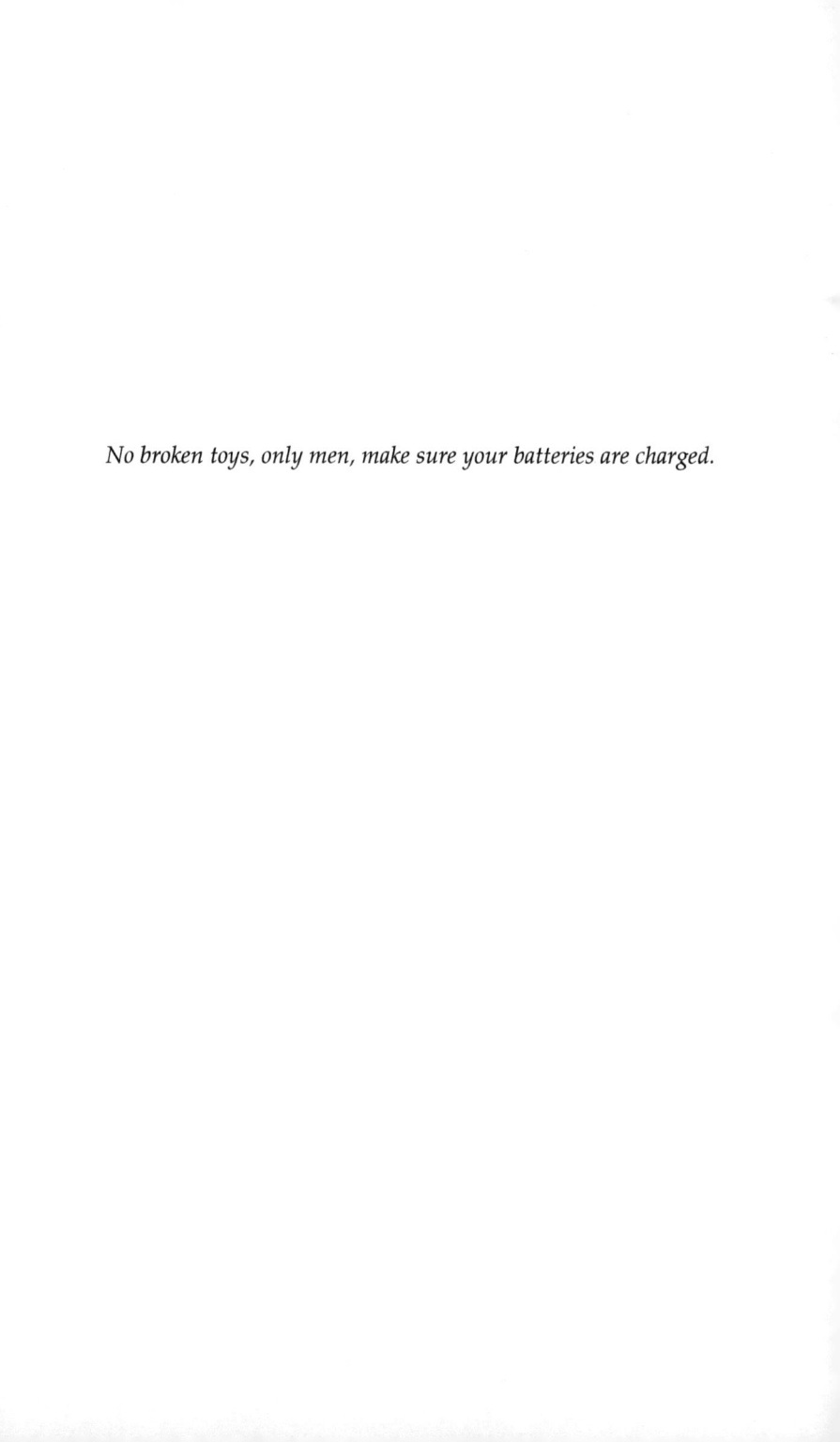

No broken toys, only men, make sure your batteries are charged.

An immeasurable pleasure lies in breaking something beautiful. Art is only crafted after pain—born from it. We are all guilty of using our own blood and trauma in hopes to leave our mark on this world.

We pluck our souls bare and throw our harvest into performance. We crack and beat our pointe shoes before giving them a chance to twirl around the stage. An untouched shoe is useless.

My pointes are beautiful because they are used. If only that grace extended to the ballerina.

The thin cracks in their soles are a mercy compared to the deep bruises in my spirit. I'm broken beyond repair. With each pirouette, a hook right in the middle of my stomach pulls me down until the earth itself opens up to swallow me whole. Some days, it seems easier to let it.

A broken ballerina is not nearly as enticing as her broken shoes.

CHAPTER 1
LYLA
INTRODUCTION

THE DRESSING ROOM buzzes with the nervous energy of twenty-five ballerinas as we filter in for auditions.

"Thirty minutes," the stage assistant calls as she closes the door behind us.

Picking a cubby in the corner, I keep my chin high and my gaze forward as I cross the room. Many of the girls hang back a moment to watch. Sizing up the competition isn't unusual in this industry, but I don't have the time for that.

There are some benefits to having been the best and failed. For one, I don't need to watch anyone else. The ghosts of my past performances are my only true competition. Every ballerina is a little hungry for success—too thin, overworked, desperate—but if they're hungry, I'm *starving*.

Judgmental eyes cling to me as I stuff my bag inside one of the empty cubbies. Pretending they're not all watching me, I quickly strip out of my sweats and climb into my tights and leotard. I'm not here to impress these dancers or give them another embarrassing story to tell about me—the broken ballerina.

I pick my leotard nervously, trying to ignore that it no

longer fits me right. Whispers burn my back as the other dancers find their spots and start to change.

"She fucked him." I don't see which ballerina speaks, but it's not surprising. I've been living with this rumor for a long time now. Their disdainful comments are nothing compared to being the broken Prima Ballerina, a woman accused of betraying her own dead mother before she was in the ground.

I say nothing. I don't even turn. I've had a long time to practice pretending I don't care, but I silently tell my mother I love her, and I never would.

The only eyes or whispers that concern me belong to Mikhail Ivanov—the producer waiting outside to cast his Christmas production.

Coming here at all shows my desperation. This is the fourth audition I've hit in the past three weeks—none of which have taken me. Not many productions have open roles left, especially paid ones. And pay is what I really need this Christmas. I understand that coming here is useless because Mikhail has good reason to reject me. Yet I have nowhere else to be.

Several years ago, he offered me a position in his company. For a couple of months, baskets of exotic fruits and impossibly colorful flowers arrived at my address with a simple note. Even today, the lines of Mikhail's notes hang heavy in my gut, much like my lack of breakfast.

I felt seen. But my stepfather is no one but Carter Livingston. I was the crown jewel of his company, and he grew jealous of the gifts and convinced me to stay. He made me promise to never leave his side.

Family.

A simple and powerful word that he threw out carelessly any time he needed me to do something.

I often wonder where I would be if I had gone with Mikhail. I don't let myself get carried away. I made my choice, and I have to live with the consequences.

The past doesn't matter. The beautiful things Mikhail said about my form aren't true anymore. I'm not the same dancer I was when he wanted me to be his star. I've fallen far since those days.

I'm doomed on that front as well. Mikhail is expecting a dancer who no longer exists.

I tie up my shoes, and the pink ribbons slip softly between my fingers despite all the abuse. That softness is one of the only remaining vestiges of my old life, and it takes a second too long to let them go. I can't let it go.

They call us one by one. My last name is Moore, so I'm dead center. The time will allow me to stretch and school my face into the perfect mask. Despite how easily I once donned it, it's hard to hold up now.

The room grows larger by the minute. Since when are there so many dancers around? I swear the competition didn't used to be this thick. That's to show how sheltered I've been.

"She's really still at this?" Someone laughs, and I'm not even sure they're talking to me. I refuse to face them and find out either way.

There was a time when they couldn't spell success without the letters of my name. Lyla Moore, the prime offering of the best theaters in the world. I hold those memories close to my chest, even if most are illusions. I never had a choice as to who to dance for, not as long as Carter had any power over me. He would never let me go in glory, only in shame.

I shake myself, wondering the same question they are. *Are you really still at this?*

How easy is it to fall from grace all because of one jealous man? How easy was it to tarnish my reputation and end my career prospects? How fast a rumor can spread.

After every hit I've taken in the past couple of years, auditioning with teen girls when I used to lead my company is the least of my humiliations. I stand tall and convince myself I'm not a failure. There's no point in dwelling on what could have or should have been. I'm here *now.*

Even if now is so ugly.

My cheeks redden with shame as my fingers trip over the small tear on the left side of my leotard. I didn't care what my clothes looked like during the good times because I had more.

I could dance in nothing but my pointe, and a full audience would applaud and call it brilliant defiance.

"Lyla Moore."

My head whips up when they call my name. The time passed faster than I thought it would, and the idea of facing Mikhail with the routine I've prepared today turns my stomach.

I can't do this.

"It's actually her."

The whispers are impossible to ignore as I cross the room, their stares like lasers burning my skin. My heartbeats and steps synchronize as I swallow the lump in my throat, looking straight ahead at the woman holding the door and clipboard instead of at them.

My hands ball into fists as I chase out my self-doubt; my need for security is greater. With each step, I promise myself this is the last chance for them to kick me while I'm down. Carter will not continue to ruin my life.

I hope my name burns their tongues.

Following the assistant out of the dressing room and across the backstage, I crack my knuckles and pray to the deities who once favored me to do it again.

Just this time. Mikhail is the only one who can put me back together.

She holds a finger up, signaling for me to wait. With a nod, I bring my hands to my waist and roll my ankles to warm them up. I've performed this routine a million times. I won't miss.

My eyes close, and I breathe in hope. The broken ballerina will dance again. They can't keep me down. I will get up again, just like the music box I had when I was a girl.

I will be stronger.

"Go in, Lyla."

CHAPTER 2
MIKHAIL
INTRODUCTION

"LYLA MOORE, auditioning for any open female role," the assistant holding the door says. My heart skips a beat, and my stomach drops in anticipation.

It's been two years since I lost out on the opportunity to cast Lyla as my Giselle, a disappointment I've yet to recover from. I remember the way she used to move, the perfection of her features, and the way she held them as she danced. I hold my breath in expectation.

Then the dancer steps into the room. She's skinny even for a ballerina, flat and unimpressive.

My stomach does a sick sort of flip.

Who is she, and where the fuck is Lyla?

My jaw tenses, and sharp pain shoots from the tip of my chin to my ear. *Fuck*, I stifle my soft groan.

The pain is worsening instead of improving lately with all the stress taking over. I rub my jaw, trying to dissipate the ache, but the poorly healed bones and tendons just creak disagreeably. My attention returns to the ballerina onstage. Lyla wouldn't dare stand me up, not after everything she's done. But is that really her?

My fingers strike the clipboard in my lap, and a nervous

ballerina glances my way, unable to make out more than my shape in the darkness. I try to force myself to relax, but I can't, not for my audience nor my sense of self-preservation—until *she* faces the room fully.

With her delicate features in view, my muscles unwind enough to relieve the worst of the pain.

Lyla.

That relief only lasts a second, quickly replaced by the obvious question. *Why does she look so off?*

The delicious hollow beneath her throat dips gauntly, giving her a starved look rather than her previous alluring elegance. The circles beneath her eyes are bruised, too heavy for makeup to hide, and her leotard is a mess, ripped on the side, pilled, and faded, like it's been washed too many times.

What the hell happened to her?

She's been missing from the dance scene and *society* for two years. Of course I've heard enough rumors about her, but giving in to the speculations of jealous ballerinas has never served me before, so I didn't give them much credit in this case either.

That changes as I take in how far she's fallen. Something must've happened to her to cause such a startling decline. They said she was in a relationship with her stepfather. An unimaginable low for someone who had just buried her mother.

A surge of jealousy courses through me at the thought of someone else touching her, especially the man who had the pleasure of her gracing his stage. It would make sense. She said no to me and stayed loyal to him. Maybe that's why.

She's beaten. If the rumors that ruined her career are true, and the relationship went downhill, that could explain why the ballerina at center stage is not the one I saw dancing years ago. Either way, her detractors have won. I never thought lowly enough of her to pity Lyla, but I'm not so sure anymore.

What have I done?

My stomach flips as I consider the years I've spent sick over the image of her twirling around *my* stage. Have I been obsessed with an illusion instead of a woman? I wrote this ballet and the accompanying score with her in mind. Hours at my piano dedicated to a standard that no longer exists? Is the thing I've wanted most in the world gone?

She attempts to keep her head back and her shoulders high. There's nothing wrong with it, but she lacks that old finesse. Frankly, I'm repulsed with myself, with her, with the institution of ballet as a whole for building these impossible dreams just to watch them crash at our feet.

Right when I'm about to give up my entire life's work, I notice the artful movement of her feet getting into third position. Her eyes fill with determination as she bends her arms, the grace and poise still present, a glimpse of who she used to be sparking to life. Every part of me relaxes and tenses at once.

The only woman who ever told me no.

A few years ago, Lyla made a big deal about her independence as a dancer and a new vision she wanted to pursue. *Daring, bold Lyla Moore.*

She planned on leaving her stepfather's company—or so she said—and allowed local directors and producers to vie for her to fill positions in their companies.

I spent months sending gifts to woo her, lavishing her with whatever flattery I thought might win her over. Eventually, she went back to the bastard anyway, continuing to dance the traditional ballets he had asked of her for years. It was a professional slight, and not a small one, but there turned out to be an even larger problem—she made me obsessed.

I'm not the type of man who wants anything on the surface—rich, powerful, connected. Of all the things I've ever wanted, like attention from my mother, or my father's approval, this one fucking dancer circles the top of the list. My heart beats so hard that my chest aches.

There's no music as she twists and turns, a weak comparison to the blinding light she used to be, but I hear the song she's performing anyway. My hands flex as I realize I've seen this before—only better.

Her body has always merged with the notes as she moves. She's never danced to the music. She's the composition lifting off the page. The notes play in each turn she takes. I hate her for that, for radiating intensity even when she's half beaten.

Pure, unadulterated poetry.

Is this *exactly* the same routine she danced for his company?

After she turned me down, I let impulse get the best of me and bought a ticket to watch her. Her perfection stayed with me, even when she performed his traditional, uninspired ballets. The hunger and jealousy were so great that I had to leave before the end. If I had it my way, I would have thrown her over my shoulder and stolen her from him.

My knuckles strain with the urge to reach out and shape her, push her toward more daring moves. She's playing it safe, only hitting the mark because she chose the easy way out. My face warps in rage as I watch. *Did she really think this was enough?*

How long has she wallowed in her own misery while her muscles weakened and her form withered? I'm consumed by rage now. How dare she dance like this for *me* and like that for *him?*

The ones who have finished their auditions sit in a row, and their whispers are far less quiet than their feet. They're discussing the ghost of Lyla, who pirouettes across the stage. It doesn't matter what she does. She'll always be the target of their gossip. I'd pity her if I weren't incredibly offended that she dared to come here like this.

Counting her ribs, I pay more attention to her lack of

muscle definition. My fists tighten as I wonder when she last ate. Is she keeping her routine simplistic because she's unsteady on her feet? Not eating because she's mourning the loss of her torrid affair?

A growl bubbles from me, scratching my throat on its way out. I pride myself on being a controlled man, but anytime Lyla is in the vicinity, my primal urges take over. I want to own her, put her name on my show bill, and be the master of her every move. I want to push her until nothing about my little ballerina is safe ever again.

Lyla stops in a final pose, and the music she created with her choreography abruptly ends with her left foot twisted at the wrong angle. The old version of her never would have allowed such a thing. The air thins, and the watching eyes expect something that won't come—a signature Lyla Moore finale.

She bows and leaves rather than sitting alongside the other dancers. I wait about thirty seconds before following her.

I'm careless by leaving, uninterested in the remaining auditions. It's always been like this. I forget everything else when Lyla comes to play. I lurk in the shadows as she crosses the halls with her head down. I'm glad she understands how badly she fucked up and hasn't lost all sense.

But even at her worst, there's something about Lyla. I've been in this game for many years, seen many productions, and enticed many good ballerinas to my stage, yet no one ever compares. I knew I had to have her the minute I laid my eyes on her. She could only dance for me.

I follow her to the dressing room, my back to the wall, watching her through the small gap in the open door. She peels off her ripped leotard and then her tights, shoving them into her bag. I watch from the back corner of the dressing room. I decide I'm not hiding, and it's not my fault she never cared to close the door.

My insides boil, and I wonder if I should confront her. Spell out to her how insulting it is to watch her dance like that when I know she's capable of so much more. The need to spare the use of my jaw stops me. The injury is permanent, and speaking isn't comfortable, but maybe she's worth a little more pain.

I've chosen about six words that will frighten her and give her the proper idea about what to expect when, all of a sudden, she's naked. My train of thought stops in its tracks with a resounding *fuck*.

Her ass is even better bare, and I have this crazy feeling I can smell her skin from here even though I know I can't. My cock presses against my zipper, and I can't remember the last time I was this hard. She doesn't turn to face me but opens her cubby and moves a few things around inside. Long blond hair spills down her back, flirting with the dimples above the crest of her ass.

The obvious hints of malnourishment concern me, but she distracts me from the thought when she grabs a T-shirt from her bag and throws it over her body. No bra, nothing.

She never turns, so the image of her breasts remains nondescript, but I picture her small tits tipped with hardened nipples from the cold air of the poorly heated room. Saliva pools in my mouth at the thought of tasting them.

She lowers her body to grab her sweatpants, and her slender thighs part just far enough to flash me her pink pussy, begging to be fucked. The moment crystallizes as I memorize the color and shape and paint myself a vivid picture of how tightly she would grip me. Then she steps into them, pulling the fabric over her hips with nothing underneath. I have to hold back the curse ready to fly off my lips.

She's going to walk around with her pussy out like that?

I don't have time to dwell on the thought. She's grabbing her backpack, so I step away and enter the adjacent room so she won't see me. I catch the smell of her perfume as she passes by, long blond hair swinging after her.

Why the fuck couldn't she make an impression like that during her audition?

I step out and go to the dressing room where she once was. I don't like that all I can smell is hairspray and perfume rather than her pink little cunt, but fuck, it makes me even harder.

I open the cubby she had stuffed her bag inside, and like an early Christmas gift, I find the pair of panties she didn't bother to put back on.

I'm not a stalker or some panty-stealing Peeping Tom, but I guess all of my standards are flying out the window today. I'm taking a subpar ballerina into my company, and I'm about to rub my dick with her panties.

I look around the room for just a moment before I crush them to my face. The smell of her cunt, her sweat, all of it draws a bead of cum to the tip of my cock. I pull my dick out and lean against the wall as I stroke myself, trading between breathing her and rubbing her leftover juices into my dick.

My breathing increases, and my grip strengthens. I bring my hand down with unrestrained anger. My desire is so powerful, yet it's the last thing I want to feel. I want to own her, but this feels a lot like being owned.

I imagine her cunt opening up for me—her warm, silky pink entrance taking me to the hilt. Burying myself in her, filling up her too-delicate body and moving her the way I like. Molding her with an artful hand until she perfectly fits all my needs.

A pearly bead of cum drips down my shaft, and my grunt hurts on the way out. I'm closer now, her panties soaked with precum, and I'm raw anger and desire.

She told me no once. And I won't let her do it twice.

The relief crashes through my body in a powerful wave. Ropes of cum forever stain her little scrap of pink. I don't know what possesses me, but I shove those cum-soaked underpants back in the cubby for her to find later. Because she'll be back this time. I'll make sure of it.

I want to stain her too, carve my name into her body, use every hole, and call her mine. I want to choreograph her dances and fuck her until her legs don't work.

I leave the dressing room with a rare smile on my lips, thinking about the outrage on her delicate face when she finds the panties.

She doesn't need to know what creep is coming for her. As long as she knows I'm coming.

CHAPTER 3
LYLA
INTRODUCTION

IT'S BEEN four years since the last time I was genuinely proud of myself. It was a production of *Swan Lake* in my last company, and I danced so perfectly that I left the stage knowing I'd never be able to do it again.

If I close my eyes, I can still feel my muscles exhausted in the way only an impeccably danced routine can provide. The ghost of my smiles hangs in my cheeks, a tightness made of exquisite pain, and the delicious trickle of sweat racing down my chest.

But now, I avoid closing my eyes, afraid the tears will run if I do. My skin feels too tight, stretched over my bones, and my jaw hurts from clenching it. My steps land heavy like my body can't balance my weight—as if I'm an alien to myself.

I didn't do well, and the desire to be my own cheerleader can't change the facts. I could lie and say I did my best, but not even the mirror would believe me.

My best isn't a hypothetical I've yet to achieve. Hundreds of people witnessed my best, and now each step is a disappointment.

I don't want to be right about my depressing future. I'm only twenty-three, so the best years of my life should be in front of me, not behind. I never got to fully enjoy the stardom. For the longest time, I was next—the next star, the next prima ballerina. I was potential bursting at the seams. Every company wanted me because I was full of promise—the face of tomorrow's ballet.

My stepfather is a marketing genius, and he made sure of that image, cultivated it from the raw material of my skill, and then just as surely, he made me nothing.

I lost my father young, and that hole in my heart left me wanting a man to care about me. A stepfather to truly love me seemed perfect, but that was never what my mother's husband planned. I only learned that when she died, and he tried to sleep with me.

My heart died with my mother, and then my soul when Carter kicked me out of his company and told everyone it was because I was trying to sleep with him rather than I rejected him.

It took a little over two years for my small inheritance to run out, enough time to lose the definition in my muscles and the strength I'd worked so hard for. A tear rolls down my cheek as I leave the stage, and I know I should have stayed hidden. Let them speculate and whisper my name while telling sordid tales. I should have gotten a job and done what anyone else in the world does.

But ballet is who I am, and I'm worse than dead without it. Carter took everything from me—from my childhood home to the empty promises of stardom.

I've spent a lot more time with the faded promise than I did the dream, and I've been nothing ever since.

That nothingness has stayed with me like a shadow stuck to my skin, like an inescapable whisper. This is only my fourth audition since I decided to come back, and for a normal ballerina, that wouldn't be much, but for Lyla Moore? What a disgrace.

My shame is bigger than me now; it carries me. I'm a sack

of bones being dragged and pushed forward, seeking humiliation. Am I trying to save my ego or destroy it in its entirety? I went from star to joke at the snap of my fingers.

When I enter the dressing room, it's empty. Every dancer has been cued backstage or is sitting in the audience watching the rest of the auditions. I breathe in a sigh of deep relief and quickly peel off my sticky leotard and tights. I'll find out how the audition went one way or another, so there's no point in waiting around for another blow.

I'm packed up, wearing my sweats, with my bag over my shoulder a couple of minutes later, but my hopes of escaping unnoticed are dashed as I step into the hallway.

"Lyla, right?"

My head whips around, and I'm looking at a smiley redhead who was definitely called to audition after me. Without meaning to, my eyes go over her shoulder to the cluster of people standing about ten feet back and whispering.

"Yes." Admitting my own name burns.

She smiles even bigger. "I watched you back at *Swan Lake*. You took my breath away." She wriggles her hands together, looking uncertain. "I'm a big fan."

I wince, but her face is open, and I fear she's sincere. That's even worse than her making fun of me in terms of the stab to my gut. I dig deep for something to say, but before I have a chance, someone from the group in the back snorts.

"Yes, Lyla. We're all big fans," a long-legged brunette says, her mouth curving on a mean smile. It takes me a second to realize I know her, but the last time I saw her, she looked more like a gangly teen than a bombshell. She's been dancing just as long as I've been, and we bumped into each other in auditions, but she never dared to speak to me.

Until now.

Flipping through options, I consider barking an insult or rolling my eyes and just letting it go. Either were fine options back when I was a real person. But now I'm a ghost, and no matter how I wish I had anything left in me to say, the words never leave my throat. The truth is stuck inside me, just like it was with my stepfather, and I don't fight wrong with wrong.

The tears fight to escape once again, but it's the last piece of control I have, and I refuse to be this pathetic.

"I loved dancing *Swan Lake*. I'm glad you were there to see it. Thank you for the compliment." The words taste like cardboard, and they sound stiffer, but I manage to smile at her before I turn on my heel and get the hell out of Dodge.

The piece of garbage I call a car sits in a parking lot a block away. Fighting with the key in the lock warms me up some, and then I struggle to get it started.

I turn the key, but all the car does is whine. My mouth closes on a thin line, and I try again.

"Come on, come on..."

My hands shake from desperation rather than cold. A sob bubbles from my throat, and I hit the wheel as I scream, "Fuck!"

It's getting snowy out there. My hands are freezing, and my knuckles are blotched white and red as I rub them together, trying to get some heat. I'm too skinny, but I don't know what the hell I can afford to eat, and I'm too tired and stressed to think.

My voice is hoarse. I've been on the edge of a cold for weeks now. My life plays like a movie behind my eyelids, but the happy ending never comes.

I was talented, loved, and safe when I was little. I had a dad who took care of me, and even when he was gone, my mom tried so hard. I was set for a future doing what I loved. And then everything was taken from me.

Voices interrupt my wallowing, and I check my rearview to find a group of dancers talking and laughing. My cheeks redden before they even get a chance to see me.

"Shit."

My desperation takes over. They can't see me like this, not after today's performance. They can't know how bad things have gotten for me. *If I'm the only one who knows, maybe it's not real.*

I try the car again, my hands shaking over the keys. *Please cross the road. Go anywhere else.*

I squeeze my eyes close and try again and again, but the car only whines, and the voices come closer and closer. My leg bounces with nervous energy, but I don't give up. I keep waiting and praying for mercy that never comes.

Their group walks toward the car parked directly next to mine. Their thick coats rustle together as they approach. A jealous surge at how warm they must be mixes with my fear and self-hatred. I consider dropping down and trying to hide, but how pathetic can any one person get?

Their voices slash my skin, and the pain is so real I can almost smell my blood dripping.

The moment they see me digs that blade deeper, their eyes moving from where I'm sitting to the mess in the back seat. The windows are closed, so I can't exactly hear what they say, but I see my name mouthed.

Lyla. Lyla Moore. Sleeping in her car.

"Oh shit," one of them gasps.

I want them to make fun of me, to be cruel, but their expressions are full of pity, and something fragile inside my very being breaks.

They avert their eyes, unable to look at me a moment longer as they all climb into the car and pull away. I'm crying once again, feeling empty inside, and like a joke, when I turn the key this time, it works straight away. I snort, shaking my head. *Pathetic.* The car sputters and trips over itself as I pull away.

Everyone in this forsaken town will know I'm sleeping in my car tomorrow.

Everyone will know how much of a joke I am.

My stepfather will know, and God help me, I don't know what to do if he comes back for me.

My jaw hurts from the pressure I'm putting on my teeth, and I wonder how I can ever reassemble the pieces of my life.

Something tells me I'm too broken to form any recognizable shape.

I don't hope anymore. I'm too raw to ever let myself believe in things like Christmas miracles. I know who I am now, and I can't keep hanging on to who I used to be.

I pull into a discount store and look for No Parking signs. This one is all clear. Turning off my car, I lock my doors. I can't afford the gas it costs to run it for the night, and I pray once more I don't die of hypothermia in my sleep.

CHAPTER 4
LYLA
ACT 1

I'M DANCING AGAIN. *Pirouette, jeté and the crowd applauds. My eyes fill with tears as their proud faces watch me. Happiness dares to blossom as I cross the stage, holding my arms up gracefully, my chin up high, and—*

A sharp tap pulls me out of another fitful sleep. My heart shoots into my throat, and my head throbs with the suddenness. I unglue my eyes, swallowing the bitter reality as the first rays of morning light peek into the car through the frost.

I'm unsure what woke me. I'm barely able to feel my toes, and my hands are locked painfully, and they're useless as I lift them. I breathe against them, except it does nothing but puff fog and prove there aren't enough blankets in the world to improve my situation.

"Lyla!" I hear my name muffled from someone's lips, and a tap on the window follows, making me jump.

Frost coats the glass, and I can't see who's outside but a blur of black. I'm not thinking straight. My heart hammers inside my chest, and I turn on the car, ready to run.

"Open the damn door." They try the handle, and this time, I recognize the voice.

Every cell of my body freezes when I realize it's him.

He found me.

Carter is here.

One of the most powerful men in this city towers over my car. The frosted window blocks his expression, but his features are a stain on my memory, and no matter how hard I try, I can't forget him. I was so careful hiding from him. I sold the car I had by the time I lived with him and blocked his number from my phone.

It didn't matter. It's like the past two years are gone, and I'm within his reach once more. Fragile and easy to manipulate. I'm back to the gilded cage he built for me. A willing, guileless victim.

Pulling my phone out of my pocket, I surreptitiously press record. Driving away won't help with someone like him. He's too pushy, too used to having everything he wants, and his hand is already on my car. My finger twitches to unroll the window a crack, but I won't dare unlock the door.

"What?" I reply, flinching as I do.

My mother married him when I was twelve. He was so attentive and tender. I was happy to find another father figure. But now, I'm haunted by the memories of the night he came onto me and ruined my entire life. My mother was barely in the ground before he was cupping my tit and telling me I was the one he'd wanted all along. I shake myself out of it, keeping my tears at bay. I lie and tell myself I'm strong.

"Lyla, I said *open* the door."

"You can say whatever you need to say and go. I'm busy."

He snorts, and my cheeks redden. I might not look it, but I am busy. I have a lot to do if I'm going to find something to eat this morning and make it to the next audition.

"This is pathetic, even for you, Lyla. Just come home and admit what you did."

"What I did?" The words escape me before I can stop them.

Engaging with him is useless. Since the moment I rejected

him, he's been on a mission to destroy my image. The whole ballet scene knows me now as the whore who betrayed her own mother. He removed me from his company, burned my bridges, and isolated me. Yet every time we've been face-to-face, he tries to convince me I was the one who initiated it. *That I'm the crazy one.*

He leans closer, the shape of his profile revealing itself and sending unbidden fear down my spine.

"You were grieving." His voice comes so soft, like when I was a kid, and he'd talk to me about hard days. "I understand that now, and maybe I should have handled you a little more gently, but I was protecting you too."

My exhaustion aches in every part of me. I've been running from him for a long time, looking for work and trying to live this impossible life. I've fought to show people I'm still a dancer regardless of the truth, but all that's left is bone-deep exhaustion.

My head rests on the cold glass, and I sniffle pathetically. "I didn't do anything. You know that."

"I might have a place for you if you're willing to tell everyone what really happened. Telling the truth has to be better than this." He gestures toward the obviously lived-in state of my car.

I didn't do anything, I repeat the words to myself, replaying the scene in my mind, ensuring I remember the real version and not his lies.

For months after, I obsessed over our every interaction, wondering if I led him on or gave him the wrong idea about my love for him. But how can a teenager give a grown man the wrong idea? A teenager who loved him as a father?

It's him, not me, and it doesn't matter if I'm the only person in the world who knows it. It's still the truth. A tear rolls down my cheek.

Would my mother believe me if she were still here?

I don't know for sure, but I'm convinced I'm no longer

safe in my car. This piece of junk has been my only refuge until now—little as it may have been.

"This is dangerous, Lyla. You're going to freeze to death. Come back home."

I dip my chin, subtly nodding to myself. I can't deny he's right. Most things about my life these days are dangerous. Last winter already featured a few near misses, and I had a more stable place to stay then and a little more money.

I hate myself on a soul-deep level as I war over my dignity and my need for shelter. Part of me wants to go so badly—give up and take my old life back. But going with him is more than accepting the humiliation of his version of events.

I know in my bones he'll try again. He wants me to come home because *I'm the one he wanted all along.* His touch still ghosts my skin, and the memory of his whiskey breath in my ear draws frightened goose bumps.

A full sob shakes me as I think about the proud girl I used to be. My head held high, a deep sense of bravery, a girl with a home who felt safe. How terribly fake it all was.

Looking at him through the frosted window, I cry harder. Losing both my parents wasn't enough. I loved him, trusted him, and then had to learn the hard way that men only want one thing.

He tried to touch me, not only abusing my trust but also warping my sense of reality. He couldn't accept my rejection. He lied to everyone, and to this day, he's still gaslighting me.

The fucked-up truth is that I still love him. If he wanted me as a daughter, I would run to his arms, but I know he doesn't.

I look down at my lap. The phone continues recording our interaction, and I don't know why I'm doing it. He'll never admit it, and I'll forever wear a scarlet letter over my chest.

A painful knot sticks in my throat. He keeps knocking. My heart hurts, and while I hate everything he did, I want to go home so fucking badly.

Just for a second, I'm about to give in. I'll live in my

house, have a place in his company, dance every night, and be warm and safe.

Before I can answer, he slaps the glass with both palms. The whole car shakes, and that dream shatters in front of me. I will never be safe again.

"Lyla, sweetheart..."

I hate the quality of his voice, as if he can calm me down and make me see reason. My head hurts, and the will to stay here and fight for what is right dissolves. *Maybe I should just end it.*

My phone pings gently. The notification of an email flashes on the screen for just a second, but it's enough for me to see that it belongs to my last audition.

My hands shake, and my fingers stumble as I rush to open it, not daring to hope, but maybe I am because I've stopped crying.

Congratulations, Lyla Moore...

I made it.

It's not a big part, but it doesn't matter. I'm going to dance again. An ugly whimper of relief slips from between my lips. My shaking hand covers my mouth, and I read the words over again.

I made it.

Carter shouts something as he slaps the window again. The mask he so carefully places over his monstrous self melts like the snow.

A small smile curves my lips as I toss the phone into the passenger seat before turning the key. The universe winks at me as the car starts without a complaint. I pull out, not worrying about his toes or his bullshit, leaving my past furiously kicking the pavement behind me.

CHAPTER 5
LYLA
ACT 1

RETURNING TO THE THEATER, I feel like a kid heading to Disney—that is if they fell off a ride the last time they were there and were traumatized for life. Excitement sizzles in my veins, the hopes of a new life, a slice of my old life. There's too much on the line today, and I try to keep myself calm as I park my car.

Rehearsals don't start for a few days, but the email said to come in, fill out paperwork, and settle in as soon as possible. I head into the theater, knowing I should be more concerned about my appearance. Ballerinas talk after all. But all my thoughts are going toward how close I got to giving up. I was at the edge of the precipice looking down while the bully inside my head was telling me to jump.

Go back with Carter.

Give up ballet altogether.

It whispered a lot of things in my ear, and today, I'm thankful I was strong enough to ignore it.

I don't want to look nervous, so I school my expression as I step into the theater. Right at the door, I find a sheet of paper leading me to the right for this season's cast, and when I follow the arrow, I dare to smile shyly, even if my hands still tremble.

Still daydreaming about a glorious return, I almost miss *him* coming my way. After all the presents and notes, we've never met face-to-face.

It's hard not to think of Mikhail as my savior, the man who literally plucked me out of the clutches of my evil stepfather. He saw something in me years ago, and he obviously still sees it if I'm here today.

I watch him walk, a good foot taller, looking sharp in an expensive suit. He eats the space between us without looking up, but my eyes follow him with hunger.

The man, the savior, the impossible director.

Mikhail is many things, but to me, he's the reason I'm still standing. It's an ill-lit corridor. I can barely make out his features, but he can't miss me since it's too narrow.

I want to assure him I'm not a mistake. I know I can be the best once again, and with him by my side, I can show them all what I can do.

He comes so close that I smell his cologne—something sinfully masculine. I shake all over and open my mouth. My gratitude is on the tip of my tongue, but Mikhail steps away from me, never looking up.

Everything shrivels and dies inside me, and I stop in my tracks, watching him over my shoulder as he disappears down the hall. It's a second suspended in time. The reality versus the dream collide in front of my nose.

I'm an idiot.

I thought he knew who I was. I thought this meant something, but I should know better than to think I have a hero out there looking out for me. I stay longer than I should standing there before I roll my eyes.

"Grow up, Lyla."

I head to the offices, and a kind woman in her fifties helps me fill out a series of forms. I hate filling out forms, but I hate even more that I have to lie. I'm not a good liar, despite what the whole town thinks. My palms start to sweat so much that the pen slides from my hand and drops to the paper.

That catches her attention, and she looks at me over her glasses. "Problem, dear?"

"Oh, I, uh, moved recently," I tell her, thinking more quickly on my feet than I usually do. The encounter with Carter still has my adrenaline high. "I just need to look up the address of my new building."

"Sure." She smiles as I pull open my phone and write the address for the local post office and then hand it over to her.

"Is there an apartment number?"

"No," I answer.

"Lucky girl," she says with a wink. Very few people in this city have a residence without an apartment number attached, and they're all absurdly wealthy. I can't blame her for my own lie, but it sits heavy in my empty stomach.

"Yeah, definitely to be cast in an Ivanov Christmas production."

"Oh, of course." She smiles like I'm a wonderfully humble and polite heiress when really I'm a liar without a home.

I smile too and step away right when more members come in. I sit over in the corner, pretending I'm not jealous they all know each other already, and finish filling up the rest of the forms. Once I'm done, I head back to the dressing room to grab a permanent cubby.

The door opens right when I reach the same cubby I had yesterday, and the cast comes in. The group from before and more. Soon, we are all here, but that sense of belonging never really reaches me. This is my home. This is where I used to feel more like myself, but now I hang by the back. I try to make myself smaller.

Of all the things Carter took from me, this hurts the most. He made me less *me*.

Their chatter fills the room and leaves me with the deepest

sense of emptiness. I worked so hard and took for granted what it really meant to be the best, to have community and be someone people looked up to. I have so many regrets that I can barely count them all with both hands. It's not fair that even this is taken from me. I came here to fight for what is mine, and I'm tired of them talking behind my back.

"Oh my God. Can you believe she made it?"

I wince and try to remember that I don't know for sure they're talking about me. I don't look their way. I tip my head and sort through my cubby.

They are nothing.

"Do you think she's on drugs? Why does she look like that?"

"Maybe she thinks he'll take her back if she—"

I swallow the colorful curse I have trapped in my throat and concentrate on what I'm here to do. Yesterday in my haste to leave after that disastrous audition, I left some clothes behind. They are still here, thankfully. It's not like I can afford anything new. I pull the dirty clothes out and slam the door shut, drawing an abrupt end to the conversation and a salacious giggle out of the girls making fun of me.

I turn around as my fingers clench the fabric in my stress, and they crunch…

The girls stare at me as I look down at my hand. The underwear in my hands are stained. There's something crusted and dried on them. It looks like someone blew their nose in them.

What the actual fuck?

I can't take it anymore. I'm already down, but they keep kicking me. I wanted to do this with the little dignity I have left, but apparently, I'm not granted even that small mercy.

I lost my mother, my family, friends, my livelihood, and the man I loved like a father. It happened all at once, and since the day Carter touched me, nothing has worked out my way.

The emotions are bubbling out of me, and I can't keep them down. My hands shake, while one still holds the horrifying crusty panties. The texture rubbing against my skin is the final straw.

"You guys think this is funny?" I ask them, waving the possibly glue-soaked fabric in the air.

This is what they think about me. I'm not a person to them anymore. I'm just something they are allowed to tease and bully. I never came on to Carter, so the fact they assume I was the guilty party and not the man who has known me since I was twelve is insane. They keep dehumanizing me, stripping me from everything so their aggression is justified.

"You're touching other people's panties, and I'm the issue? Fucking creepy," I spit at them as I turn on my heel and decide to get dressed in the bathroom.

I throw the underwear in the trash and shake with rage as I change. This juvenile prank went too far. They seemed surprised I was back but not that surprised if they left something for me to find. What was the point of that? To remind me of my past? Believe me, I will never forget.

I wish I had chosen a different cubby. I wish I said more. All the things I left unsaid for the past two years are trapped inside me, waiting to come out. I mouth them to myself when I'm alone at night and sleep doesn't come. I rehearse them more than any choreography. I have so much to say, yet I fear no one will ever listen.

People are cruel, I tell myself, shaking myself off after getting dressed.

Things are never going to be the same. I'm not the same Lyla from before, and today was my wake-up call. They will always look at me like something that needs to be squashed.

I grab the rehearsal schedule and find there's a sheet to sign up for solo time in the studios. I scribble my name for a few hours each day until they officially begin. I will prove myself to them all. They will swallow everything they ever said about me.

And no one is taking it away.

CHAPTER 6
LYLA
ACT 1

HOLD FOR A COUNT OF TWO, *push off into a single pirouette.*

Too-weak legs try to land gracefully in fourth position, but instead, I trip on my own feet. Today is a pre-rehearsal where we're learning our routines. We have two days to nail the moves before the official cast rehearsals begin, and I get to humiliate myself in front of everyone.

The extra practice times I booked were not enough. My teeth grind together. Shame warms my cheeks, and I have to school my expression as I struggle to ignore my shortcomings.

It took me years to become the best. I can't expect to get it all back in a few days.

Sweat drips down my chest, but I don't have a second to myself. Eduard, the dance instructor I met only an hour earlier, claps—a language all ballerinas understand. My back shoots straight, and a breath later, we return to start.

Step into a tendu devant, transition into an arabesque.

I'm just another body, no longer getting one-on-one coaching. I caught a glimpse of the prima ballerina earlier, the same mean brunette who teased me in the hall, and I bit my bottom lip so hard, I tasted metal in my effort not to react. I couldn't help but watch.

Her routine is inspired, stunning, and brave. It is everything I wanted to be and never could be in Carter's stale old company. My heart ached as I watched her move. How desperately I wanted to perform the moves myself. But I couldn't even kid myself to say I was prepared for them.

I walked away with my shoulders two inches lower. She might be a bitch, but it's not her fault that my best days are over. That honor belongs to Carter.

Attitude, assemble.

I didn't have to focus this hard before because my routines came as natural as breathing. Another bead of sweat slips down my skin as Eduard narrows his eyes at me, unhappy with my performance. How could I blame him when I agree? I caught him watching me a few times over the week, never with anything but annoyed questions in his eyes. He doesn't want me here. Desperation is the only thing keeping me going. Pushing forward is the last thing left to do.

We've only been at this for an hour, and my ribs feel like they're carving up my internal organs. I'm not used to hours-long, rigorous training anymore. My legs tremble, but I hold my chin up, feigning dignity that left me a long time ago.

I'm unprepared for this production, and I'm not fooling anyone. Weeks have passed since I sat down with a square meal. I'm not starving, per se. I'm just malnourished, overworked, and depressed, but I can't voice any of that, so I keep my mouth shut.

Chassé forward, extend into a grand jeté.

A sloppy landing means my joints complain as my feet stomp the floor. The noise horrifies me and draws the attention of everyone else. Eduard claps his hands loudly once again. His sharp look cuts my back, and his disappointment hangs in the air, but he doesn't say the words.

For that, I'm grateful.

"Again, from the top," he says.

We scurry across the room, our arms curving in third position for the start. Eduard rolls his fingers to his assistant, and the music plays again.

Plié, jetté.

I'm focusing so hard on the choreography that I might as well be alone when the room's temperature seems to drop. Despite the exertion, chills run through me and freeze the air in my lungs.

My hands still over my waist as we *pas de bourrée*, and my eyes find *him* through the mirror.

Mikhail Ivanov.

I've seen him multiple times this week, yet he never looks my way. The memory of his notes are something I'm not quite ready to let go of, but he's bruised my ego again and again since I became part of the Ivanov Ballet Company.

That all changes when I least expect it. I gulp, my heart hammering inside my chest when I realize he's not ignoring me anymore. I shiver, wishing I had accepted his ambivalence. It feels much safer than his notice.

His black suit and shirt cling to his body like a second skin —the devil himself with slicked-back dark hair. His blue eyes are pale like glass, and his jaw is defined and ticks when he looks at me. Something coils inside me. A chill runs down my spine, and I feel even weaker. I don't understand the ripple in my stomach as I go from ignored to the center of his attention.

The walls of this theater whisper horror stories about the impossible director. This week, I've heard no shortage of them. His attention is like a laser, painful and intense. I should have listened to the warnings because after a week of wishing he looked at me, now I know I can't handle the alternative.

The moment stretches dangerously as our eyes finally meet. Goose bumps explode all over my skin, and his nostrils flare. I feel naked under his stare, and rather than focusing on my routine, I'm devouring him. He's doing the same in return, but I don't know what he thinks of his meal.

His eyes follow me when I move into a pirouette. I use him as a fixed point, only taking my eyes away for a second as I twirl, just to be back again. My land is smooth like my old self, and I gain a little confidence.

Breaking our eye contact seems like a smart move, but I can't. He hasn't bothered with watching until now, and I want to show him I'm a worthy show. Quickly, I'm myself again. My movements are fluid, my steps sharp. I know what I'm doing, and excitement bubbles inside me just to end in a terrible crash when I miss a step. His eyes narrow, and disapproval rolls off him.

I blush, but I don't give up. I swallow hard and pick up my pace, trying to keep up with the other dancers who are now a half step ahead. My lack of breakfast is already affecting my balance, and the excitement I felt just a moment ago seeps through my fingers.

We finish, and it's uglier than my first try. I'm a half beat late. Mikhail's hand balls into a fist as he stares at my pointe, and he only stops to turn to Eduard with a questioning expression.

Eduard nods respectfully, but fear flashes in his eye as he claps and shouts, "Again!"

We all go from the top. Someone turns up the music, the crush and swell of the orchestra shakes me, and I unglue my eyes from the mysterious director so I can focus.

They say he never talks. In my opinion, he doesn't need to open his mouth to say exactly what's on his mind. His glass-like eyes cut, and his dark eyebrows express more than enough. He takes over the room, and it's like I can't breathe. I want to do it for me, but now, I want to do it for him too.

When we finish once again, the assistant stops the music. A gasp gets stuck in my throat when Mikhail steps forward onto the floor. The dancers vibrate with tension as he moves between us, their positions held perfectly, but fear fills their eyes. Their muscles are much stronger than my own, and I shake with exhaustion as well as fear as I wait.

His black shoes echo across the wooden floor as he approaches. His hands stay clasped behind his back, and his simple displeasure sucks all the air from the room.

We wait like statues for his judgment until he utters only a single word.

"Out!" His deep voice vibrates through the room with an animalistic growl.

None of us needs a second command. Everyone, including Eduard and his assistant, jumps to obey.

Mikhail remains in position. His body is the only thing between the group and the door. Dancers weave around him to escape, and I'm ready to follow them, but I don't take more than two steps before his warm palm splays over my stomach, stopping me in my tracks.

I don't react at first, the fear festering inside my chest growing and growing with each heavy second. Slowly, I glance at his long masculine fingers touching my leotard, the heat of his skin burning me. His thumb toys with the humiliating rip I managed to sew up but still leaves a pucker. His touch is even more intense than his stares or the notes he sent me when he wanted me to join his company a few years back.

I toyed with the idea of being his for long enough. Even when my stepfather said I would hate being under Mikhail, that he was too demanding, I still wondered how it would feel to be close with someone like him.

I don't have to wonder anymore. I know with every molecule of my being that I might not survive Mikhail Ivanov.

The dancers are quiet, but I know the gossip will run fast through the halls this afternoon. Their palpable relief sinks in my stomach as the last one leaves and closes the door behind himself.

It's only me and the impossible director.

Seconds tick by, and he doesn't say or do anything else, so I'm forced to move my eyes up to his chest over the black suit, finally craning my neck to face him completely.

I regret it immediately.

His nostrils flare as he stares at me like the greatest disappointment to ever bring down his company. His eyes are like the winter sky and cut me to the bone. I'm shaking, and every muscle of my body screams for release, but I grind my teeth together and refuse to fall at his feet.

I know I'm a sad echo of the Lyla I used to be. I understand my shortcomings better than anyone. If he thinks he's the most disappointed, he's in for a rude awakening. I'm my worst critic. No one hates me like I do. My missteps play back like a movie inside my eyelids every time I rest my head on the pillow.

"Barre," he says as he moves so quickly I'm left unbalanced. His low timbre travels down my spine, bringing chills with it.

He's at the barre, waiting for me, and I hurry to do as I'm told. I swallow dry and bring my chin up as my hands fall to the barre. My feet find second position—heels pointed inward, and feet spaced at shoulder width.

I don't spend more than a moment without his touch. His warm palm runs over the small of my back, and with a small push, he urges me en pointe—balanced on my fully extended shoes.

My nose turns up high as I raise my body like a good ballerina. My body is eager to do what it's meant to. My muscles shake. I need to stop and eat something before I can do this properly, but I can't say that to Mikhail, so I endure. His icy gaze hardens. How can he see my discomfort? I'm not doing *that* bad a job hiding it.

His free hand scratches his chin, the slight tightening

around his mouth and the corner of his eyes say so much, but I don't dare wish he'd speak the words. I know I can't bear it.

He taps lightly on my right leg. I drop to my heels and bring that leg over the barre, leaning on it to show how flexible I can be. I don't want to be pathetic. I desperately want to be good. Something has to make him happy with me, proud. Hell, I'd settle for him not regretting his choice.

"Développé," he growls, and there's a roughness to his voice I can't place. Why does he sound like he's in pain?

Mikhail watches my form attentively as I pivot and stretch my leg behind me, lifting it over my head and holding it in position. My back is straight, my leg gracefully extended above my head, and my skin burns as his eyes trace me. I try to look myself over in the mirror and correct any minor mispositioning.

I can't see what displeases him, so my anxiety ratchets. The intensity of his gaze and his touch do more than drive me to excellence. Heat travels under my skin, warming my cheeks to a blush and traveling lower.

As a ballerina, I've schooled myself not to fidget and move needlessly, but that's all I want to do under his gaze. I hold myself erect, squirming internally as I wait for him to look his fill. The need to please him is like a third person in the room.

He shifts his weight until he stands fully beside me, and I don't need to turn to watch his face in the mirror.

He's looking at me like an instrument he needs to tune, and I'm terrified I'll tremble and ruin his work. Mikhail's hand curves over my waist once again, and the other reaches under my stretched leg, slowly going from my knee to my inner thigh.

His hands remind me of an artist cupping the shape of the sunset, but I'm no blinding star. I'm a burned-out disappointment.

His hand skates closer to the heat that's been steadily

growing, the slick flesh that's as hungry for his touch as I am for his approval.

Tingles rush my skin. He's so close to my pussy, but I know he's not thinking the same things I am. I'm the one thinking things I shouldn't. His fingers track my skin in a confusing way, moving from my knee back to my thigh—high up my thigh. I can't say I understand his coaching. Climbing fingers aren't as universal as a sharp clap.

I'm so wet that if he comes just a little closer, he'll touch my damp leotard, and I'll only have myself to blame for that humiliation.

His hand grips my waist a little harder, and his eyes find mine.

I can't breathe.

I can't move.

Slowly, the hand on my leg makes the path again to my thigh. My nipples pebble, and I beg a God I don't believe in to please make sure he doesn't see the hard points.

His hand never stops, never returns to my knee. He braves closer to my pussy. His fingers skate over the damp fabric, and he pauses for a half beat before pressing forward. I want to die because he knows.

He knows.

CHAPTER 7
MIKHAIL
ACT 1

I CAN'T STOP TOUCHING her, and I know I should have five minutes ago. Maybe I shouldn't have touched her at all. But when my overeager fingers find my little ballerina sopping wet? There's no hope of turning back.

My cock thickens, a slow simmering desperation that's been growing more frustrating by the day. I always knew I found her attractive, but I didn't realize I wanted her this badly.

You don't think of goddesses as touchable and fuckable. I always considered her this high and mighty figure, greater than a goddess even, something I could pose on my stage if I managed to convince her.

I never imagined her looking up at me like I'm her absolution while her little cunt weeps for *me*.

I should deny her like she denied my stage, but I don't have it in me to ignore what's already in my hands when I want it this bad.

I'm a careful man, neat, tidy, so I don't understand myself as I slide the leotard aside and dig my fingers roughly over the fabric of her tights, feeling the hot, wet part of her cunt. *Fuck, I can feel her heartbeat.*

A quick gasp slips out of her before she's silent again. Her expression in the mirror gives nothing away. Does she want this? Is she afraid of what will happen to her if she puts a stop to this?

Maybe I should care, but I don't. Controlling myself isn't an option as I slide my fingers back and forth, finding her clit through the fabric.

The faintest whine echoes from the back of her throat as I roll my fingers over her. I don't need any more encouragement than that sound to shred the fine fabric of her tights separating me from what I'm owed. The subtle tearing sound fades to the wet dip of my fingers entering her.

"Ah," she breathes as I find her G-spot and apply light pressure. She's so tight, so hot, I need to bend her over and fill her with cum before I lose my mind, but I just manage not to.

"Sloppy," I tell her, insulting both of us. Finally, she notices what's wrong with her reflection and changes the angle of her foot. As she twists her hips, she gives me better access to her. Funny how fingering her little cunt has her paying better attention to her form.

She's so thin I can practically feel my fingers inside her as I start to move, first stroking in nearing motion, then sweeping her in wide circles to stretch her cunt wide enough for another finger or two. She's so tight I wonder when she was last fucked properly, and I'm desperate to give her what I know her body needs—cock and some damn food.

She holds her expression, finally giving a solid performance, and my cock hardens so painfully I feel lightheaded. Her perfect little tits form the most tempting peaks under her leotard, and my free hand moves to them. I take one between my fingers, rolling and watching her face as her flush creeps up her neck.

If she's trying to prove a point, it's finally working. She can impress me.

I want to taste her cunt, her tits, but then she'd know how

badly I want this, and our little learning experience would fly right out the window. I like her working her hardest to impress me. She might grow soft if she knows how affected I am.

I pick up my pace at the thought, spreading her lips with my index finger and pinky as I slip the middle two inside her and rub her clit with my thumb. Her heart pounds, the rhythm of her jugular obvious with how goddamn thin she's gotten.

I take her silence as a challenge and work with her more intensely than I've ever tried to finger a woman. If not for her flush, pounding heart, and white knuckles on the barre, I'd think I was failing entirely.

But then the most beautiful cry echoes from the back of her throat. Her cunt pulses around my fingers, and she comes down my wrist with a wet splash. Her face relaxes into the perfect expression, the one she used to wear so effortlessly as she danced—euphoria.

I watch, waiting to see if she breaks, if she lets her exhausted body fall like it's so desperate to. She holds it for a count of ten, and then I pull my fingers out and take mercy on my very favorite new toy, but my palm is full of blood. For a minute, I wonder if she could actually be a virgin. I shake it off, wiping my hand against my pants. She's probably just starting her period.

CHAPTER 8
LYLA
ACT 1

HE TAKES his fingers out of my pussy, deliciously slow, and they burn on the way out. I've never done anything like this, and my cheeks redden with the sinful wet sound that echoes through the room. I manage to hold back my moan of well-used pain.

My heart pounds, and the blood rushing in my ears leaves me disoriented. There's supposed to be some form of post-orgasmic clarity, but all I feel is mind-numbing confusion.

We both look down, seeing his fingers painted in red, dripping my blood down his palm as proof I never allowed any other to touch me like he did.

He raises an eyebrow in question, but I can't say a word.

Why does part of me like the sight of him marked in my blood? Why does some carnal urge call me to paint more on his skin? That's not *me* talking. I rarely think about sex, let alone something like that. I'm still horny, achingly so, and I can't expressly understand why my body so fiercely craves more when I've just come, but this need to be fucked pulses in every part of my body.

"I expect more." The words are harsh both in sound and meaning.

Does he mean my dancing? Or am I supposed to drop to my knees and suck his cock and have sex with him? Is this all I am to him? The ballerina whore?

"More," I repeat the words numbly. My mind and body war with one another.

I blink as I try to connect with myself and understand how I could have allowed this to happen, but all I see is clear blue eyes like glass, cutting and unapologetic. What is it about him that's overtaken all of my good common sense? Why am I still poised in développé?

He nods for me to relax my pose and then watches my ass and exposed pussy as I bring my leg down. The sight of his eyes trained on me makes me shiver. I try to stand straight and maintain my composure, but his gaze weighs a million pounds. I adjust my leotard and search for anything to say or do, and I can't deny that part of me hopes he might step forward, either to ease my embarrassment or touch me again.

He makes no such move, and I don't let more than three seconds of my humiliation pass before I spit, "I'll do better," and run from the room while avoiding looking into those stupid eyes. Too bad I can't take his bloodstained fingers or the last twenty minutes with me.

My attempt at escaping my director is juvenile at best and might result in my removal, but I can't stop myself. If this is a situation like the one with Carter, where sex is expected to have a part in his show, I'll find something else. I won't be toyed with like this. I dedicated my whole life to ballet, but men always have other ideas. Carter, and now Mikhail. They want more than I'm offering, and I'm tired of asking how high when they say jump.

I run straight into the dressing room. My feelings are a mess, but one thing I know for sure. It doesn't matter how turned on I am right now, I can't let Mikhail or anyone else treat me like a whore without my permission.

I'm here to dance, not to fuck.

So why haven't certain parts of me gotten the memo?

When the door closes behind me, my hands tremble. A flurry of emotions races through me, and I have the damnedest time trying to figure out how the hell I'm going to navigate my life. Thankfully, no one is back here. They were smart enough to flee the building when Mikhail opened his mouth to speak. My heart beats so loudly that I can feel it pulsing in my ears.

Wetness drips down my legs from the hole he made in my tights, and the tender skin aches where he spread me. The image of him watching me through the mirror while using his fingers will be inked in my memory for as long as I live. I'm even needier as I picture it.

I'm confused, turned on and, as usual, a mess—only this time, I have *nothing* to wear to rehearsal tomorrow.

Resting my head on the door, I groan and wonder how I can ever move on from this. Did he do that to me because he's heard the rumors? Was he as insanely turned on as I was, or is this all a game now? He's the producer. He's the one everyone jumps to please. He can afford to play however he wants, but I can't. My life is on the line. This is more than a dream—this is my survival.

So what are you going to do if sex is all he wants? Say no? Die in the cold?

I squeeze my eyes closed, feeling like a failure once again. I know I'm not in the best shape, but I thought I could do better with a production like this. I want to be the old Lyla. This is my chance to go back to the top. It's not fair that I'm here wondering if I made the cast just because of what he thought he could get from me, and worse, I'm not stopping him.

Tomorrow, I have to come in here and face everyone like this humiliation didn't happen. Like they weren't right about me all along. I pray to the gods who have forsaken me that no one heard or saw anything more than my sloppy routine, that they all ran away scared before they could see what other messes I'm capable of. *I had no idea I could squirt.*

A curse flies past my lips in my embarrassment, and I shake myself off. There's no point in staying here, but where the hell am I supposed to go? Back to my car to sleep.

Quickly going to my cubby, I grab myself a change of clothes. I pull soap and shampoo out of my bag and clean myself over the sink like I've been doing for the past week. Scrubbing out my hair with the hot water takes time, but it feels pretty amazing. It's not comfortable exactly, but it's good, like I'm human or something.

The temperatures are forecasted to drop yet again tonight, but I can't do anything about that. I dry my hair as thoroughly as possible so it won't instantly freeze when I step outside, but it's still going to get a little crunchy. This is necessary, though. I can't show up at rehearsal looking dirty and worn out—the thought stops me in my tracks. What the hell am I going to wear tomorrow? It's not like the tiny rip on the side I can sew up. My leotard is bloodstained, and I can't imagine a patch job would go unnoticed there.

Dear God, what am I going to do?

As I stare at myself in the mirror and dry my hair, I think about all the dancers gossiping about how the director called me out. People who hate me will have a great time thinking that Mikhail himself tossed me out on my ass. No one knows I got an orgasm out of the deal unless he's planning on telling them. Will I ever find someone who wants me for the right reasons? Tears threaten to come, but I don't have time to feel sorry for myself.

I finish with my hair, so twisted up and humiliated that my cheeks are flaming despite my lack of an audience. I put my stuff together and step out into the hall, keeping my head down. I'm lucky I haven't been caught washing up here, and I know I won't have a chance tomorrow with the tight rehearsal schedule.

"Hey, Lyla," a feminine voice pulls my eyes off the floor I was so carefully inspecting. One of the friendly dancers waves at me with a coffee in one hand. "Staying late too?"

I want to answer, but my tongue is too big inside my mouth to greet her properly. So I just shake my head to let her know I'm getting the hell out of here.

I pick up my pace, pulling on layers of outerwear as I go. I'm at least three times thicker than I was a few minutes ago, and my hands are warm as they close around the knob. I open both doors at once. I sigh in relief at not having to answer any more questions, but it quickly turns into fog and anxiety as I step into the freezing December air.

The wild wind lashes my exposed skin, so powerful it's like knives. I step back, trying to protect myself in the hollow of the door, and at that moment, it sinks in that I can't sleep in my car anymore. I have lived in this city my whole life, so I know its winters well. The day was coming, but I hoped I had a few more weeks. Last year, it didn't get impossibly cold until January.

A frown puckers my brows as I close the theater's doors, my heart racing for a whole different reason. The ballerina who told me she's staying late has taken up residence in one of the studios, and she doesn't notice me as I follow my way back to the dressing room. There's an old couch sitting on one side and a pile of stunt pads for when we want to try out more adventurous moves on the other.

I grab my phone and scroll through the local resources for the homeless. I try to avoid using them as much as I can because I'm too scared of being so vulnerable beside strangers. I have options. *Don't I?*

I find the answer to that question is no. There isn't a person alive who's on my side. They all believed Carter. I haven't had a real friend since before my mother's funeral, but I guess if they're all gone, I've never had a true friend at all. I lower my expectations and try the shelters, but they're fully booked for the next two weeks.

My head cast down, I place my elbows on my knees and stare at the floor. It doesn't matter how long I stay. The magical solution never comes. Eventually, the music ends, and the friendly ballerina heads home without making another stop in the dressing room. I appreciate that I don't have to choose between hiding or lying.

The cleaner comes around soon after, throwing an uncertain smile at me before she removes the trash and goes through a small door I never paid much attention to. She fiddles around for a few minutes before returning and leaving the dressing room.

Excitement lights my blood as I hang back about ten feet and follow through the small passage. It's long, at least forty feet, and I find myself getting nervous as I wind down the hall and around the back of the stage. There's a flight of stairs to the left, and I take it. I could go up to the offices or down to what could only be the basement. I choose the route less likely to feature security cameras.

The stairs are too loud beneath my feet, and I work to silence them. My excitement clogs my throat as I find there's no door, and the wet heat of the furnace wraps around me. The basement is covered in mechanical stuff, old boxes, and dust.

The only light comes from the emergency exit signs, and there's a dankness to the air. I enjoy the stale, warm atmosphere for a minute before realizing it might even be too warm. Exhaustion instantly swamps me.

Stepping into the center of the room, I find a clear space. My bag slides down my shoulder and lands on the floor. Silence passes as I listen carefully for a sign of anyone down here. The only interruption is a rat, quickly running from one wall to the other. My heart sinks. *I can't sleep here.*

The thought of heading back outside to face the cold is even less appealing than the rats.

I could wait here, I suggest to myself as I check the spot on the floor directly beneath me and sit down with my knees by my chin. My teeth fiddle with my lip, possibilities fueling my imagination. I could wait around until the cleaner is gone and sneak back into the dressing room, set my alarm early, and be up and dressed before everyone comes in.

I could use the time alone to practice.

The idea is beyond dangerous. If I get caught, I fuck the only job offer I've had in months, and that's *if* Mikhail doesn't decide to have me arrested.

But my hands aren't hurting from the cold for the first time in forever, and I know it doesn't matter how risky it is. I'm doing it.

I need this.

Watching the floor for more rats, I stay quiet until I know it's safe to go upstairs.

CHAPTER 9
LYLA
ACT 1

LIKE I IMAGINED, the place is deserted, and I breathe happiness so deeply it's more like soul-shaking relief. Part of me wants to practice, to push myself into the ground until I'm good enough for Mikhail, but how am I supposed to do that when every part of me still shakes from his fingers, when my tights are ripped, and my leotard is bloody?

I curl up on the pads because I can build a little wall and hide in case someone unexpectedly comes inside. My layers of outerwear become my pillow and blanket as I build myself a comfortable spot. The alarm is set on my phone. I decide the theater might be haunted as I fall asleep listening to soft and haunting notes that disappear every time I try to focus on them. Dancers' feet and swishing fabric that fades whenever I say, "Hello."

Truthfully, I'm not sure if I ever speak or if I just think the question as I slip away into another realm. Fear seems like a foolish reaction; the ghosts of Christmas past and I probably have a lot in common. I'm happy at the thought that I'm not alone, that other things are trapped in ways they can't comprehend, just like me. Misery loves company, especially at Christmas.

I don't mind when the alarm goes off. It's been a long time since I've gotten this kind of warm and mostly relaxed sleep. My body feels more capable and strong than it has in a long time.

I'm up early, wearing my sweats and lamenting over what I'll do today when I take my bloodstained leotard to the sink and start scrubbing. The tights are a lost cause, and I pray I can find a pair to borrow if I can't get the blood out.

I've made a pretty good attempt at it when the ballerina who complimented me the first day comes in. The leotard hangs over the bench, and she looks at it with a raised brow.

"I spilled coffee on it." I roll my eyes and facepalm.

"I have a spare if you need one," she tells me as she puts her bag down. Her name is Maeve, and despite her choice in friends, she might be my personal angel.

I swallow the emotion out of my voice as I answer. "I think I'll be okay with this, but I could really use a set of tights."

"Yeah, of course," she answers as she pulls a set out of her bag and tosses them to me. "Hey, Lyla, want half my donut?" she asks, already breaking it in half and handing me a piece. "Save me from myself," she encourages, and I don't even pretend to turn it down. I'm too hungry.

"Maeve, I need to ask you a really big favor?"

"What's that, Lyla?"

"Please don't tell anyone about the tights."

She gives me a kind look and nods before continuing to chat about her morning and her issues with Eduard.

"I swear if Eduard makes one more face looking at my thighs, I'm going to bring a donut to eat

in front of him. You're lucky you're so skinny." Her eyes skate over me with longing, and her desire is like a stab to the heart.

I want to tell her it's crazy she thinks that this is ideal when I'm like this because I'm starving. There's a difference between a healthy body and mine. A huge difference. Why the hell doesn't anyone in this industry see that? I know I used to be part of the problem, but truly lacking it has changed many of my opinions about food and, more importantly, dancers' bodies.

I shake my head, clearing my anger and a flicker of guilt.

"You're doing great. Eat whatever you like, and he can get fucked."

She giggles. "*We're* going to be fucked if we don't get changed."

Chatting with someone while getting dressed for rehearsal is like a flashback to another life. We head to our cubbies at the same time, and my eyebrows push together when I see there's a package inside mine. My hand closes around the brown paper.

I slept in the dressing room. When the hell did this get here?

I breathe hard as I wonder who dropped it off and when. Did they really not see me? They must not have, and I did build up a wall to make myself harder to spot. My frown distorts my face in my confusion. I look from one side of the room to the other as if I can find some clue or hint as to when it happened. I don't think the ghosts are buying gifts.

I peel back the brown paper, revealing silky tissue paper that slides through my fingers, and I open it with shaking hands. The fabric inside matches my skin tone precisely. It's so correct that the choice alone feels intimate, but then I touch it and feel the quality. This gift is obscene. This isn't something you give to someone you consider a whore.

Before I have time to hide, Maeve is looking over my shoulder.

"Oh god! They are gorgeous!" She smiles. "I guess you don't need to borrow anymore?"

Mikhail sent me a brand-new leotard and tights. I blink. It's the only thing that makes sense after what happened. There isn't anyone else left alive who would buy me a gift.

It's been a long time since I put my hands on something so beautiful. My rational side wants to find out what he expects for these. Are they a transaction? Is it a gift? All he would have to do was say they were the latter, and I would open my legs for him again.

Did he leave them here himself? The idea of him sneaking into the room while I slept sends shivers down my spine, but he never would. He's far too important to run an errand like leaving some clothes in a ballerina's cubby. But the idea that he could have, that he might have been so near me again while I was so vulnerable has me aching all over. It's funny how the things I fear most are desirable when Mikhail is concerned.

I change into the new attire, and they fit me like a glove. There's something so thrilling about the perfect way they grip my body and the precision between the color of the fabric and my skin. It's as if he's touching every bit of me. Grabbing my water bottle, I take one last lustful look at myself and follow the rest of the dancers to the rehearsal. *He dressed me.*

When rehearsal ends and everyone leaves, I find a sandwich sitting on the bench in front of the cubbies. I don't feel nearly as guilty as I should when I snatch it up and take it to the basement while I wait. Not a single girl here couldn't replace a sandwich, and this one looks especially good.

I wait in the basement, stuffing my face like the thief I am, until finally, it's silent except for the few ghostly hints of music that always disappear when you try hard enough to listen. Once I'm sure it's clear, I return to the rehearsal room. Last night was an exception, not the rule. I'm not just here to pass out somewhere warm. I finally have a place to practice, so I'll be worthy of this gorgeous fucking leotard.

Even alone, my cheeks burn when I place my hands over the barre. A full day has passed, and Mikhail was nowhere to be seen at rehearsal or after. There's no reason to flash hot with desire at the memory. It's even stupider still to hope he might show up and give me an encore.

Get it together, Lyla. That's not what you're here for.

I skip the music, choosing to let my mind wander and meld with the choreography. Starting the routine, I get it wrong straightaway, missing a step. It's embarrassing and frustrating. *I expect more.*

Mikhail's words play on repeat in my head as I push myself harder. I fall and hit the ground hard, but I stand and do it again and again. The clock is ticking, and I have no choice but to push as hard as I can or give up, and giving up means letting Carter win.

My mother's memory doesn't deserve that.

It's past two in the morning when I call it quits and go over to wash myself in the sink and change my clothes. I plan on waking up in less than three hours, and I briefly worry I should have finished up sooner and given myself a little more time. That type of sleep schedule never bothered me before, but I can feel how worn down I am, more so than I thought possible.

I pick through the cubbies until I find that someone left an apple in theirs. It may be stealing, but who wants a pest problem? I eat it while listening to music.

I climb into my pile of stunt pads and build the wall to hide me even more carefully this time. No one saw me last night, so they shouldn't see me tonight. I'm humming to myself when I fall asleep.

Day after day, it goes the same. I eat better because the ballerinas always forget some food item or give up on it to keep their figures. I wait for someone to wonder who is eating the dressing room food, but that never happens. They simply don't care enough to even ask.

My routine is improving, and Eduard doesn't look so disappointed when he critiques me.

This situation is the answer to my prayers. I'm always

warm, I can practice, and I'm safe from Carter. I'm easily a better dancer than I was a few weeks ago, and my cheeks are even rosy. My body is still dangerously thin, and I'm worried about what might happen to me long-term if I don't find access to stable food soon, especially with how hard I'm pushing myself physically.

I go to the laundrette one afternoon, clean all my clothes, and get more stuff from my car. I leave enough behind in case Carter is watching, but I have a few good items with me.

Including my pajamas, which I fall asleep in with a silly, hopeful smile on my lips.

CHAPTER 10
MIKHAIL
ACT 1

I'VE WATCHED Lyla like it's my job for the past week, forgetting the company and most of my other responsibilities. My assistant is beside himself, my junior director close to fainting.

Rather than worrying about them or my responsibilities, I'm leaving food for Lyla in the dressing room, like the theater doesn't have rats, and generally keeping tabs on her. My attention doesn't go unnoticed by the other ballerinas or anyone else.

But Lyla? Whether she notices or not is an ever-shifting mystery. One thing I'm sure of is that she hasn't noticed me watching her dance late at night.

She barely looks at me since I fingered her over the barre. Her first week here was an amazing power play of feeling her eyes on me and choosing to respond by ignoring her, like she'd done to me. It's possibly a moot point, given I've masturbated at least fifteen times to her since. Now I feel we're too evenly matched, and I wonder again why I need to be infatuated with someone like her.

At night, her lack of attention is fine. I like to dissolve into the magic of her body, and she dances better when there's less pressure. This is especially maddening during the day when she often performs like pure shit. If I didn't think it would make things worse, I'd have cornered her already and forced her to tell me what she's thinking.

I'm sure she doesn't see me, and I'm so insane with it that I might snap until I catch that same flush creeping up her neck and always when I'm near her. Lyla notices me. If she's trying to build my interest and drive me insane, it's working.

Morally, I'm concerned I may have fallen far enough that I'll never recover, and still, that seems like the least of my problems.

Snow falls all around my driver and me. My breath fogs the windshield because I refuse to sit in the back seat and be driven around like an infant. Every moment in a vehicle sets my teeth on edge, my forever-broken jaw screaming with the ghost pains of the accident that changed everything. I hate driving with a passion. It reminds me of so many things I'd rather not think about. The cold has set in deeply, the weather reminding me of that time.

I don't bother to question whether or not the snow will stick. The cars and foot traffic will pack it down and dissolve it soon enough, but a grungy brown-white coating of it will stay stuck to the city long past Christmas. It will look like this for months...

We're parked in front of the fucking downtown post office all decked out in holly jolly splendor. Lights line the whole building, and a giant, inflatable Santa and reindeer decorate the front lawn. This is *definitely* not where Lyla lives. The falling snow gives everything the appearance of being trapped in some absurdist snow globe. *Why did she give a fake address?*

"Boss, I don't think—"

I hold up my hand, stopping him. The sting of the obvious does not need to be rubbed into my face right now. My driver has been with me for years. He's a good man and doesn't interpret my gestures as rude.

He knows my panic sits just beneath the surface of my calm exterior. I'm not as bad as I often am when we drive. Oddly, how fucking angry I am is actually helping me to manage it. I'm here, in the car, for her, and I'm outside the goddamn post office. There must be a reason they call it going postal.

My hands flex. The heat pumps from the vent, but it's having a hard time keeping up with this chill. Fat flakes of snow fall over the glass ever so gently, and a violent image of blood and glass on snow flashes through my head.

Rather than sinking into the feeling, I tuck it away. Dropping my head into my hands, I try to focus on my next move. I'd walk the block and knock on every door if I thought it would help, but none of the buildings on this street are residential. *Why did she give a fake address?*

When I pulled out her personnel file with the intent to follow her home, I thought it was a new low for me. Really, it was just the beginning of a chain reaction of lows designed to humble me and make sure I have no ego left to speak of. How else could you explain two grown men at the post office with no packages in December?

My driver and I stay parked outside the post office for another fifteen minutes, and I'm not sure which of us is more confused as to what the hell is going on. The post office never magically turns into a house, and eventually, I make a spinning gesture with my hand, signaling for us to return to the theater. If I'm going to find anything, it will be there.

"To the theater," he says, giving me a chance to protest but not demanding a response. We turn it around and head back uptown.

I've waited for everyone to leave for the past week and then found her dancing. The first night filled me with so much pride that I nearly stepped out of the shadows to tell her what a good girl she was. Instead, I watched. I quickly became less pleased when I realized how much work she really has to do. Enraged seems to accurately describe my current state, and I know where to find her.

Regret isn't one of the many emotions flying through me, though maybe it should be. This is hardly acceptable behavior; two wrongs don't make a right. But how can I have true regret for my actions when her health has improved from my attention?

Lyla's physique is strengthening and filling back out, meaning she's been eating the things I've left for her. With more calories, her practice is translating to muscle development. Those late-night practices won't go to waste, and that's needed because we're closely approaching the beginning of our Christmas season.

I'm probably a shitty stalker, and I'll admit I've given up before her every night this week, gone home after convincing myself it would be so much worse if she saw me. But each night I watch her, my need for her grows more intense, and her determination leaves a warmth in my stomach even the winter chill can't chase out.

She wants to give me better, wants to be better. But then I remember the goddamn post office…

I should have known better. Casting a girl who's so malnourished she can barely dance might have been the beginning of the chain reaction of lows, but maybe not. I wonder what point I went from observer to irrevocable fool, chasing her to a fake address. I should have left her memory on the stage the first time I'd seen it and ran. Of course developing an interest in something so beautiful would end in pain.

The post office confounds the issue of why she's not eating on her own, rather than explaining it. If she's willing to eat the food I leave for her, why the hell isn't she seeking it out? She must know she needs it, that I need her to be healthy. The shows are sold out, and it wouldn't do to have a disappointing ballerina on my stage, no matter how small the role.

I can't for a moment pretend she's not made a fool of me. In so little time, she's taken over everything. I can't think about choreography because, in the back of my mind, I worry about how thin she is. I'm not at the theater. I'm driving back from the damn post office.

I've made very little progress in stalking her. You'd think that would be the least my obsession could manage, but no. Never did I imagine I'd be wishing I was better at following women home, but Lyla not only brings me to new lows, she digs them for me. How does someone as wealthy, connected, and successful as me *fail* at stalking someone?

Maybe it's a matter of luck. I'm more an opportunist than a hunter? I haven't found her all alone in the dressing room naked again, and what I've found online has been dated and less than helpful. But I'm getting tired of the placid, upper-crust approach. It's time to get hands-on.

I return to the theater and head straight upstairs to the offices where the security cameras cover most of the building. It's a central space for the directors and producers contracted here, but it's not *my office*, so I can't stay here indefinitely.

I flip through the camera angles until I find Lyla in one of the rehearsal rooms. I'm briefly pleased before I realize I'm still furious with her. *What would the fucking IRS say when I tell them my ballerinas live at the post office?*

As I watch her dance, voices echo on the stairs leading up. Standing in front of the security camera display, I might have noticed them, but I was too busy watching Lyla, coaching and correcting her from here. Smiling slightly when she seems to hear me despite the impossibility of that.

"It's going amazing. Don't worry about it," a deep male voice says. I don't realize I recognize it until the door opens, and I find none other than Carter Livingston and his director.

Both men freeze momentarily, staring briefly before Carter pushes into the room.

Gray hair frames his face. His flat brown eyes focus on me with a spark of malice that wasn't there the last time we spoke. I say nothing for a full minute, and neither does he. It's rare that someone forces me to speak first, but very well.

"Are you lost?" I ask, trying to keep the worst of the bite out of my voice. As far as he knows, we're competitors, but we have no reason to dislike one another. It probably wouldn't help my reputation to growl at him even though I'd like to.

"Not lost at all, Mikhail, looking for the light maps."

I raise my brow at him in question. *Why the fuck would you need those?* I ask with my eyes, and this time, he fills the silence.

"Our rehearsals start next week. It's such a shame Lyla wasn't ready. She isn't fit for this production yet, but I guess she might be good enough for yours." His tone says he cares for her, but his eyes have a predatory shine.

I'm not sure how he heard the news I cast her, but I can think of about twelve people who would have taken the time to report back to him. I don't say anything, and there aren't enough words to describe what I'd like to say, but I do consider punching him. He may have tradition, but he's more than lacking in vision.

Instead, I nod at him agreeably. She's not good enough for mine either, but that doesn't matter right now. We still have some time, and if her rate of improvement holds steady, she'll be just fine for my show.

"She begged, you know, to come back to me. People saw it, too. I know you're a proud man, Mikhail. Do you want to be second choice when she's not half the dancer she used to be?"

He's trying to manipulate me, but it's working. Did she beg him to come back? Are the rumors true? My blood pressure rises as I clench my jaw and fire pain through my system. He winks at me, and the sensation is like oil coating my skin. *Slimy bastard.*

He finds the plans he was looking for.

"Ah, perfect." He hands them to his director and half turns back to me. "I'll be seeing you, Mickey. Who knows, maybe if you can get her back into shape, I might take her after all." The two of them head down the stairs.

"Don't fucking call me that." I manage to unlock my jaw a moment later, but they're already on the stairs, their steps and conversations far too loud to hear what I have to say. Potent rage sinks into every part of my being, and I'm not sure who will suffer most for it.

Carter Livingston is hosting his Christmas production in this theater. The man she danced for, possibly fucked too, will be here with his company. The same one she was tossed out from. And he might try to win her back.

He can't have her. She's mine.

CHAPTER 11
MIKHAIL
ACT 1

A MILLION THOUGHTS run through my head as I take up the position I've used all week to watch her. She steps into the room after some time, and I wonder what took her so long tonight. Jealous thoughts that she and Carter had an encounter of some kind run through my head as she turns on the music.

Her body grows more delicious by the night, and I don't know why this jealousy is burning me half to death and making my cock hard. Her routine is improving, her form regaining its grace.

Hours pass as I watch her work her routine into the ground. She's almost good, passable at least. Is this all for him? Did she have some advanced warning he was coming here, and she wants to improve herself for him?

Potent rage fills me as I realize that like a fool, I allowed myself to believe her place in my company was what changed her. That she wanted to be excellent for me, not for him to take her back. I believed I was enough for her, but all of this was for him.

I'm combustible by the time she finishes. Her elegant body is slicked in sweat, and I'm more animal than man as I stare at her. Sense and reason left me several hours back, replaced by jealousy and a primal need to reclaim what's mine.

Is she really mine if she runs back to him so quickly? I ask myself again and again. And what the hell would I have to do to prove the point to her that she does?

She returns to the dressing room. The sink runs for awhile before she reemerges in her oversized t-shirt. Normally, I would just enjoy a chance to look at her, maybe touch my cock again, but I'm wondering about her wet hair and what the hell she's doing.

She heads over to the stunt pads and snuggles into them, quickly falling asleep.

A soft snore kicks up, and I'm sure she's out. I step into the room, unsure what I feel, but its intensity can't be ignored. Why the fuck is she sleeping here? Is she homeless? Is she waiting for *him?* Questions assault me as I stare at her, trying to figure out what the hell is going on here and why it makes me so sick.

She rolls over in her sleep, flashing me her little cunt, and it's bare again just like when she put on her sweats. When does she wear underwear? Does she know what she's doing? At least twenty people have keys to the front door, and she's lying there with her pussy spread like a pretty pink buffet.

The urge to show her what can happen when she's so negligent overwhelms me, and my tongue aches even worse with my desire to taste her.

My cock is harder than it's ever been. For hours, my sense of reality has blurred as my carnal need for her has grown. I've been wanting her for years, watching her for countless hours. I fucking need her, and she's lying here with her cunt out.

She's dancing for him.

My cock is in my hand. I can't take the pressure, the intensity of it all. My balls clench, and my cock leaks like fucking her is the only thing they've ever needed.

How dare she sleep here? Endanger herself and give him another chance? How could I be stupid enough to go home before her every night?

I'm sitting on the edge of the pads. She's spread wide open, pretty pink perfection—I really can smell her this time. Enough light seeps from the bathroom to illuminate her silhouette. My cock jumps in my pants, and I touch it to keep from going insane.

My teeth dig into my bottom lip as I try to control myself. Rather than developing my strength, it tears to shreds as I reach out and play with the spot her pussy lips join. She sighs in her sleep like she's dreaming pleasant things. My touches remain soft, and I wait to make sure she's still asleep before I spread her lips and feel her silky smooth cunt for the second time.

She's so pretty, her blond lashes fanned over her cheeks, heart-shaped lips softly opened and pouting. Blond hair fans across the pads and the balled-up sweatshirt she's stuffed under her head.

Her tongue darts out to taste her lip. She sighs, and her hand lifts and drops, resting against one of her perfect tits. Lyla is everything, and I want more—need it. Playing with her clit, I release my throbbing cock so I can slide her shirt up her body. Goose bumps break out over the skin on her stomach as the shirt moves, and a moment later, her little tits drop from the fabric.

Fuck, she's perfect. I need her.

She hasn't woken up or shouted for me to get my fingers off her. Her soft little moans mean she wants this, and I don't give a fuck that I know better on every level. I'm not thinking clearly enough to care about better or right as I lean down, cock in hand, and part my lips slightly, cringing at the creaking sound it makes and the ensuing pain. I find both worth it as I suck her nipple into my mouth. The taste of her skin is absurd pleasure and salt. My being vibrates, and she moans low in her throat, but her eyes don't so much as twitch.

I play with her clit with the tip of my cock, and I can't hold back anymore. She's all I ever wished for. She tastes so good that I keep hurting myself and stretching my jaw just for another taste. I'm leaking precum. She's so wet, and when I play with her entrance, all she does is whimper and turn her face to the side.

She's worked her body so hard she's practically comatose. All that practice is needed. She's finally getting better, but I never imagined this as a benefit. Lyla is a series of doors I never thought myself capable of opening, but something about taking what's mine has me insane.

She's mine.

It's that simple. She was mine the moment I saw her dancing for the first time. Leaning against her, I crack my jaw open and wrap my tongue around the stiff peak of her nipple. The pain is worth the experience. My cock strokes the line of her pussy, and I close my eyes in pain because I can't go down and feast on her.

I groan, imagining the taste of her pussy, drinking from her while she comes all over my mouth. I drive myself crazy, my desires officially beyond my body's capabilities.

I'd injure myself for a taste of her.

I'm making a mess of us, both wet and wanting. After every sleepy moan from Lyla, I think she's waking up, but she's having a long wet dream. I let go of my cock and graze my thumb over her slit until I reach her clit and slowly circle it. Her leg twitches, and her hip goes up in search of friction.

I give my little ballerina what she wants.

I work on her clit, my mouth opening carefully for another forbidden taste. Between her breasts, she smells like roses, something delicious and feminine. I shake with the want taking over me, the need to devour her reaching new levels. I want everything from her.

I want her dancing, her cunt, her whimpers, and her future.

My teeth graze her nipple at the same time as I dip two fingers inside her. She takes me in, so snug it feels impossible that my cock can fit inside her. I bring them all the way back out and push them slowly in again. Her hips follow my movements, and the whimper she lets out is sinful. It comes out raspy and from the back of her throat.

I almost come all over both of us. It's too much, and I can't take a second longer. I take my fingers out of her, and she's so needy. Her hips keep moving, wanting more. I grab my cock, spreading her wetness all over me, and I play with her with my tip, the warmth and softness drawing a groan out of me. Fuck, it hurts, but if anyone's going to get this response from me, it's her.

Repeating the motion, I slide it up and down her cunt. The silky slip between us is intoxicating, the sensation better than some of the sex I've had. Spreading her wetness from her clit to her opening, I forget that either of us are human.

We're less and more than that at once. We were meant to do this. Lyla was meant to be mine. Her soft moans in her sleep are all the confirmation I need. My little ballerina was born to take my cock. I'm going to come inside her because she's supposed to take my cum.

My cock is pressed against her entrance as I talk myself up to what I know I'm going to do anyway. I know what I'm doing is wrong, but the idea of her belonging to Carter and not me has a grip on my sanity. She can't ever dance for him again. She can't even be around him. He doesn't understand the gift she is. I do. I won't wait around in the shadows while she trains for him. She belongs to me now.

My cock goes in, slowly stretching her. She's so intensely tight I can't help but curse. I haven't spoken so much in years, and here I am, hurting myself over her pussy. My jaw strains and aches, but it fades quickly to the pleasure as I slowly slide my entire cock inside her. She whimpers and whines, her body and walls twitching around me. This is everything I didn't know I needed. It's better than having her on my stage.

A whine builds in the back of her throat as she takes me. I fill her with my length and enjoy the feeling of my head filling her to the hilt. Holding her in place, I thrust short and hard, building up a pace that has her body bouncing back against me. I pull out and watch the sight of me entering her.

I start to worry that maybe she wasn't starting her period. Perhaps she's a virgin after all. Am I really taking her virginity while she sleeps? I don't know, but I should pull out just in case. I don't. I just thrust my hips, sinking deeper inside.

I thumb her clit, waiting for her to wake up. I know she's going to. She might be tired, but she's not dead. She's already moaning like I've broken her out of the deepest parts of sleep.

I'm too close, about to embarrass myself inside her when her eyes flutter open. She can't see me well in the dim light, and when she opens her mouth, she says, "Oh my God, Carter, please stop."

Hearing his name from her mouth while I'm inside her is my worst nightmare. They were fucking. Why else would she assume it's him?

A noise builds in her chest, and I think she's about to moan for *him*, whine for *him*, just like she practiced and danced for *him*. But instead of that moan, she sobs.

"No, no, no. Please. Carter, stop. I don't want you!"

I recognize the desperation in her tone as she struggles. She shoves my shoulder, anxious wheezes shaking her chest.

"Please," she begs again, and it all clicks for me. I grab her face as she cries, shoving deep inside her. I should stop and leave her alone. But I'm not sane when it comes to Lyla, and there's not a chance in hell I'm going to pull out, letting her think she's squirming on Carter's dick.

"It's me." The words ache as I force them out, but she needs to hear them.

She struggles for another moment, but her tears slow. "Mikhail?"

The moment stretches, and I wait for her reaction to my touch. It's me. Not him. Never him.

"Thank god," she whispers and frantic fingers grip me.

The world stops.

She fucking clings to me like I'm the answer to her prayers and not the monster in the shadows. Her arms lift to circle my neck, her legs wrap around my hips. Lyla buries her nose into my neck and inhales my scent.

"It's really you," she breathes.

I don't remember anyone being happy to see me. Not my parents, who were never loving. Not the ballerinas, who are always afraid. I grew up ignored, so I made sure to never be invisible again. They recoil when I face them, *and* they respect me, but not one of them holds affection for me. They don't consider me *safe*.

Lyla holds me like I'm her everything. As if the legends of my terror, and my personal poor behavior aren't a bother for her.

"I thought, I thought—" She shakes her head, and the end of that sentence lingers in the air.

She thought it was him inside her, and the fact it's me is a relief. I'm not sure how I could behave so badly and still receive such a compliment. Lyla Moore feels safe in my arms. I fuck her shallow and slow, but I need more. I put space between us and look down at her, catching her outline in the dim light.

"He started those rumors about you." The truth fills every part of me. "You never slept with him."

"I've never slept with anyone."

The words are a salve. It's not that I treasure purity when I'm anything but; Lyla's actions are only a concern because I am so deeply obsessed. She's mine in every way. No one left in this world bears a physical connection to her.

It's sick to think her lack of parents could be a good thing, and I know that, but they leave a wide-open playing field for me to be Lyla's everything. I need that more than I need air. Her producer, her director, her first. For once, my dreams seem attainable. They just come at her expense.

I wrap my hands in her hair and adjust the angle of our bodies until she's loose and open, taking me like it's her God-given destiny. If I thought Lyla was art on the stage, she's everything as I take her.

"Mikhail, Mikhail," she chants my name, and it sounds like she's reminding herself who she's fucking as well as begging. I'm only too happy to oblige.

I press an aching kiss to her lips as I search for just the right angle to set her off. She returns it, sweeping her tongue out to meet mine. I can't exactly return the favor, but there's something delicious and carnal about her licking me this way. My need to taste her overwhelms me and fills me with nearly as much anger as Carter's words, but my jaw is already screaming from sucking her nipple into my mouth.

I pump my hips into her. All the anger, need, and longing I've spent the past three years nursing like a bad addiction, slipping away. Her pussy shakes around me, squeezing and tensing, and I know I'm done for.

"Mikhail," she starts to chant as she builds to her orgasm. Careful to keep my rhythm exactly the same, I keep my cum in my balls as I wait for her to tip over the edge. The moment she does, sweet moans spill from her lips. I follow her, pumping her full of more cum than I thought myself capable of producing.

I'm a new man, the pleasure erasing all the pain, and my lips form the only word that has consumed my dreams and nightmares for the past years.

"*Lyla.*"

CHAPTER 12
LYLA
ACT 1

"GET YOUR THINGS."

Those were the last words he spoke to me, and I'm not sure when he's planning on blessing me with another. I pack my bag as he watches, eyes narrowed distrustfully at me, though I'm not sure what *his* problem could be, given I'm the one who woke up to him inside me.

His watch is too attentive as I put my few possessions inside the canvas, but he never asks where the rest of my belongings are, and I'm relieved not to have to tell him.

He knows far too much already.

I hold my old backpack against my chest as we head out to the car. The wind whips me, cutting through my layers with wicked efficiency, but the cold doesn't sink so deep as the silence. He hasn't said a word to me since the rehearsal studio, and that, mixed with the postcoital adrenaline, has me nearly shaking.

Snowflakes fall, Christmas lights flash and shine, and we're alone on the street for a half second before his car pulls up to the curb, sloshing wetly and muddying the snow.

The silver paint job sparkles despite the poor weather, and

the windows are tinted so dark you couldn't hope to see inside. I step forward to open the door for myself, and Mikhail reaches out a hand to stop me. A beat passes before a suited driver climbs out and walks around the car.

"Good evening, miss," he says as he opens the door for me. "Sir." He nods to Mikhail. My silent director nods to him, still without speaking, and gestures for me to get inside first.

The warm air from the cab overwhelms me as I climb in, sliding over the leather bench and taking the farther spot near the window. I rest my head on the cool glass and sink into the softness of the upholstery. Mikhail gets in behind me, and his driver closes out the last of the chill. He's older than me, maybe Mikhail's age, with some gray just starting to show. The air is thick and warm now, and my breathing slows down.

"Home, sir," the driver speaks without question but waits for Mikhail to protest. He doesn't, and we pull out into traffic.

My fists squeeze that backpack like it's my lifeline as I watch the snow and city blur past. Christmas decorations and lit-up window displays give the strange mood in the car an overly festive backdrop.

Out of the corner of my eye, I catch his leg jiggling with nervous energy. The car is filled with both his and mine. His knuckles whiten as he grips the fabric of his pants, and my brow furrows with so many questions, but I'm too afraid to look and discover I'm the source of his stress.

Why the hell is he taking me home with him? He never explained, and there's so much pressure in going with him without some assurances. I want to ask for them, but the request catches in my throat. His thoughts are the thing I'm most interested in but also most afraid of, and I'm too fragile right now for how they would tear me apart if they were unfavorable.

My hands shake, and I don't know if it's the virginity I just lost or the prospect of going home with Mikhail—which I'm still not sure why he would ask. I'm so desperate to know what he's thinking I eventually chance a look at his face and instantly regret it. He seems more uncomfortable than I do. His lips are held too firmly, and his skin is as white as a ghost.

He looks... afraid.

Why the hell would Mikhail be afraid?

I'm quickly discovering a lot I don't know about him, and so much of what I assumed is just blatantly wrong. My image of him was that of a director too full of himself to waste his time even looking at those beneath him. The few words he's spoken in my presence have sounded difficult.

There's a painful grit to it, and clearly, he avoids speaking when he can. He must have a reason. Just like he must have a reason to be so uncomfortable in his own car. I open my mouth to ask, but the question dies on my tongue as I realize just how nice of a car we're sitting in.

Mikhail has more money than I realize, I decide as I take in the emblems and special details. The car heads uptown into the ritzier districts as fast as the traffic will allow. I should have known since he sent me enough gifts. He dresses like a moody print model, and that doesn't come cheaply, but the reality of how far apart we are is cemented for me.

He pulls his phone out of his breast pocket and starts texting. The coldness of the action shocks me. Do most girls get cuddles after their first time? A rawness sets in, and I just want him to touch me. Mikhail doesn't strike me as someone who gets awkward after sex. No. That's all me and my stupid red cheeks.

My thighs hurt as a reminder of what just happened, and my cheeks burn. I could ask him why he found me sleeping and considered it an invitation to fuck me, but I'm too chicken to face the fact I loved it, that I came with him. Just thinking about it makes me full of want again. The second I heard his voice, the world clicked into place for me.

The safety I felt in his arms confuses me most of all. I

relaxed with him, let my guard down, and believed that with Mikhail there, Carter couldn't touch me. My pussy was needy, and he fixed my problem. I needed a place to stay, and he's bringing me home. He must live somewhere nice, and I came around his cock. Clearly, I'm getting a lot out of whatever this deal is, so why does it have to be more complicated than that? I tell myself it's not and that it will be fine.

I chance another look at his hand. His knuckles are blotched white and red now, gripping so tightly he's wrinkled his designer pants.

Something is wrong.

Warmth travels from my chest up to my neck. It's a mix of desperation—an emotional one to get close to him and the physical need to rub my legs together. I'm craving more sex already, and I'm not sure how to process these feelings since they are entirely new to me.

The one person who ever tried to touch me before Mikhail was the man I considered a father.

That experience left me feeling so unclean and guilty even now. *What would my mother say?* I cried many nights, taking long showers and scrubbing my skin in a fruitless attempt to erase that night. One hand on my breast, and for two years, sex has been the last thing on my mind.

Mikhail awakened something inside me. Even before I knew it was him, I was dreaming about him. In my dreams, we were back at the barre, and he was barking delicious orders. He's the most confusing man in the world. I feel wanted and rejected at the same time, but I can't stop myself from wondering what he's thinking. I want to know what's on his mind. I want to soothe his soul. I want to hold his hand and give him what he needs the same way he makes my desires a reality.

I can't change the fact that I feel like he needs me. It might be stupid. Maybe he doesn't at all. Or perhaps he's just as lonely as I am. Maybe I can fix it.

I'm just about to reach out to *him* and make sure he's okay when the car slows to a stop outside one of the most famous tourist attractions in this city. I glance through the window for the first time, finding the iconic stone edifice in front of us.

He lives here?

CHAPTER 13
LYLA
ACT 2

THE MONUMENTAL BUILDING sits in the heart of uptown. Each Christmas season, it transforms into a winter wonderland, decked out in what must be millions of lights and ornaments every November to January. The huge Christmas tree sits right out front.

The gothic-style building itself was carved from sandy-colored giant stone and is impressive, to say the least. Garland, lights, and bells hang from every dramatic architectural point, and a clock face sits in the center of the very top. The sweeping hands tell me I've long since turned into a pumpkin.

The thick snow falling is the finishing touch of this perfect Christmas painting. The car pulls up right outside the building's entrance, a set of large golden doors with a revolving one in the middle. Dramatic red carpets start on the sidewalk and lead inside. A doorman rushes from his podium to greet us.

Mikhail doesn't wait, opening the door and climbing out first. The older man stands beside us a moment later, dressed well in a suit and hat that give him the impression of a service position while still looking suave.

"Mr. Ivanov." He dips his chin, but Mikhail ignores him as he offers me his hand to help me out. I want to call him out for being rude, but then I remember he doesn't talk—*most of the time*. It's incredibly evocative when he does. I smile at the man myself before looking back at Mikhail.

For a suspended second, I stare at the long fingers that have been inside me. The air freezes inside my lungs. My heart races in my eagerness to touch him again. He's warm and masculine. I'm obsessed with the feeling of his fingers inside me.

His palm is soft and large. The length of it spanned my entire back when he held my waist. He made me feel tiny, desperately feminine, and not in the way that usually frightens me, but as if I could fit perfectly against him.

My conflicting emotions battle inside me for a moment too long, but ultimately, I take his hand. Our touch is brief, like a whisper, but butterflies explode in the pit of my stomach as I step into the street with his firm hold helping me out of the car. When I look up at him, his eyes flash, saying something I don't quite understand.

The wind blows in my face, and his hand is gone, the absence stinging. The sensation of his touch lingers on my fingertips just like it does on all the other parts of me. I take in the gorgeous Christmas decor and try to make sense of all the ways I've been wrong about Mikhail Ivanov.

We walk through the glass doors leading into the foyer with white tile, gold accents, and vaulted ceilings with stone arches. I find myself underneath the most beautiful crystal chandelier hanging from the center. Just like outside, Christmas slaps me right in the face—trees and white lights, silver and gold bows, reindeers, and lights. Everything looks expensive and magical.

It's so beautiful that it fills me with the most heart-wrenching sadness. When Mom was alive, Christmas meant something. She loved gift-giving, and she was the best at wrapping them. She loved this sort of thing and would have been thrilled to come inside. Grief grips me by the throat, but once again, it's not the time. All I want is to grieve in peace.

We cross the foyer with his presence guiding me and his hand floating near but not touching me. An attendant presses the button for the elevator as we approach. We step inside the most spacious elevator I've ever seen, mirrored with gilt panes that match the rest of the building. He's still not looking at me.

Is there a reason he doesn't want to? Does he regret what he did or forcing me to come with him? Thoughts of Christmas with my mother make me homesick. The damnedest desire to be held aches in every part of me. I think about the notes he wrote for me when he was trying to bring me to his company and his reverence for my craft.

Those notes were as frightening as they were evocative, and no matter how good I was, I knew I couldn't live up to his belief in me. Disappointing him was the only option, so I never really considered that offer. Somehow waiting this long has made things worse. It won't stop there. Slowly but surely, I'll prove to him I'm unworthy of all the chances he's taken on me and the attention he's forced on me.

I'm a failure, homeless, and soon, I'll be all alone *again*.

I study myself in the mirror and flinch at the woman staring at me. My blond hair hangs dry and lackluster, and my sweater dwarfs my wrists, highlighting their boniness. I'm flushed, but it doesn't look healthy.

I count how many ways I look horrible, but Mikhail interrupts my thoughts as he reaches out and takes a stray lock of my hair between his fingers. Once again, our eyes meet through the reflection, and I turn to him with a question in my eyes.

"Snow," he says simply.

His hand drops a second later, and he steps back as if he can't be found that close to me. I bite my lip. I don't know if I have the right to be hurt. I don't understand enough of our dynamic to form expectations, but I must have, judging from the stab to my heart.

Floor after floor, the tension threatens to devour me. Finally, it stops on the top floor, the button marked P lit. The wide doors open, exposing the most beautiful apartment I've ever seen.

"Holy cow," I blurt as he steps into the foyer and waits for me to follow him. The elevator beeps, urging me to leave, I think... *Jesus*. I step out onto dark hardwood floors that span the foyer and extend to what I can see of the rooms beyond.

He heads into the apartment, and I follow him for a lack of anything else to do. If the rest of the building is a Christmas wonderland, this is the opposite—stark, white, industrial-feeling lights, brickwork, and leather couches. It's still the most beautiful space I've ever seen.

But then I gasp, and my backpack falls to the floor. *That view*. I run to the floor-to-ceiling windows facing what must be the most exclusive view in this city. The giant tree out front looks tiny from here, like a miniature. The popular ice rink shines a few blocks over, the colorful lights flashing across the empty ice.

My breath catches as I realize how high we are, as if nothing can touch us. The enormous tree looks tiny from this distance, and it isn't the only thing miniature. The world looks more harmless than I've ever seen it. How could anything so small ever hurt me? The street below is just like looking at a snow globe.

The skyscrapers and the people with their dreams are all just little ceramic figurines. Dots of lights flickering through the sky reflect off the fat snowflakes like the swirls when you shake the globe. I touch the glass, wishing I could extend my hand beyond it. The wind blows, and the snowflakes execute the most incredible choreography.

"Is this where you do the thing?" I ask, fingers still poised against the glass.

He doesn't reply, *of course*, so I turn around. His glass-like eyes are fixed on me, and I wish his thoughts were as clear as those eyes. I blush, clearing my throat. He doesn't look interested in my jokes, but maybe he just needs his hard shell cracked.

"You sit here and look at the little people while you plan world domination?" I raise my brow at him, and I'm shocked when I realize I'm flirting. Wasn't losing my virginity less than an hour ago enough for me? I rub my legs together surreptitiously as I realize it's not.

No laughter, not even a pity smile. I try to hold his gaze, but it's too heavy and says too much, so I let mine drop to the floor.

"Let me show you to your room." He turns on his heel and leaves me to follow.

"My room?" I ask, but he just keeps walking. "My room, Mikhail?"

I pick my backpack up and follow him down the hall of his dark penthouse, realizing he has no intention of explaining himself. Occasionally, a light glows, but it's so ambient that I worry about how I would ever find my way back out. Maybe he's counting on that. He clearly doesn't care to turn the lights on and show me around.

As he leads me down the long, dark halls, all sorts of insecurities pick me apart. *What did he think when I said Carter's name? Does he believe the rumors?*

I want him to know the truth, why that moment meant so much to me, and how safe I felt with him. It's ironic, given I shouldn't feel safe at all with a man who would fuck me while I'm sleeping, but I do. I've wanted someone to hear my version of events for so long, and now there's even more ambiguity around the truth.

I want to clear the air, but the words don't want to leave

me. This spot in his company was supposed to be my new beginning, not a confusing tether to the past. Maybe it doesn't have to be. Maybe Mikhail would believe me.

Hope dares to bloom inside me. I'm usually smart enough to nip it in the bud, but I'm warm, safe, and so relieved and exhausted I can't even think straight.

Mikhail leads me up the stairs and down another long hall. *How big is this place?* He leads me to the very last bedroom and enters ahead of me to turn on the lights. I follow him, all types of expectations forming as I hungrily take in the huge king bed.

Mikhail moves around the room, pulling out a line of remotes and placing them on the bedside table. He doesn't bother to explain what they do. Next, he moves to a dresser where he opens a drawer and shows me a stocked line of women's pajamas. Jealousy courses through me for a minute before I look and find that they're in my size.

"Wow." I'm not sure if I should be touched or creeped out, but I find I'm the former as I finger the warm, dry, silken material. I can't wait to put them on, but not before I shower. There are two doors, and I suspect one is a bathroom.

All the comforts denied to me in the past couple of months are back within my reach, and my stupid eyes fill with tears. Like every window I've seen so far, the bedroom has a great view as well. I walk over to them to avoid letting him see my tears.

I appreciate the farthest bedroom now that I see it allows me a full corner of windows for a view. It's just as lovely as the one downstairs, but with the addition of the bays in the distance and lovely ships flashing.

I bite my lip, trying my best not to look as pathetic as I feel.

It's a great room… amazing actually. It doesn't have much personality, but the view makes up for it. I'm touched and a bit suspicious, but most of all, I'm hungry for Mikhail. Why did he bring me here? I turn to him and find he's already made his way to the door. A sting of rejection hits my gut before I can tell myself I don't care.

I shake my head, looking down as I steel myself to say something without letting that hurt show. I have a chance to sleep in a comfortable bed, and I don't want to ruin it.

"Thank you. I really appreciate—"

I look back up, but he's not at the door anymore. I swallow the words but not my tears as I sit on the bed. It's so tall that my feet dangle off the edge.

I can't stop myself from wondering if this wasn't a huge mistake.

CHAPTER 14
LYLA
ACT 2

I WAKE up in a panic as blood-curdling screams echo around the room. My heart races. It's still dark, and my mind hasn't caught up with my surroundings. I sit up fast, thinking I'm still at the theater and likely in danger.

I stop myself from jumping up when I realize I'm wrapped in soft sheets, not my own ratty blankets. The bed doesn't smell like stunt pads, and the air is comfortable, not oscillating between hot and cold. What the hell is going on? *Is Mikhail okay?*

I rub my eyes, trying to make sense of the room in the dark. Finally, I adjust to the faint glow of the city beneath my window. I push back my covers and find a pair of slippers beside the bed. The screams have stopped for the moment, and my hands shake, concerned that something awful has happened to the first person to give me a chance since my mom died.

My tangled hair is still damp, leaving marks on the silk nightgown I chose, making me feel even more vulnerable. I took that shower I promised myself and nearly immediately passed out. I've always been a heavy sleeper. It's even worse now that I'm malnourished and exhausted.

Not even when Mikhail was on top of me earlier did I get up that fast. I debate for a second whether or not there's anything I can or should do to help, but eventually, I pluck up my courage and tiptoe down the hall.

It's exactly like it was when he led me here, which must have been a few hours ago. Despite the noise, the scene hasn't changed from what I can see. The hall is dark and empty. I look around, trying to find signs of light and a reason for the noise, but it's so quiet I'm not even sure Mikhail is in one of these rooms.

I keep going back in the direction we came, glancing down the stairs and wondering if I should risk it or just return to bed and pretend I heard nothing. After glancing down the stairs to be sure someone isn't lurking in the shadows, I give up and turn to go back to my room.

A raw scream tears up the quiet night, sounding even more terrified than the one that woke me. *Shit, Mikhail.*

I flinch toward the source of the noise and realize I went too far. His screams come from just a little down the hall. It must be his room. I'm certain it's his scream. My feet make the decision my head should, and I'm at his door before I can think better.

To my great surprise, the knob gives easily under my fingers. I'm prepared to launch myself at an attacker or whatever I need to do to keep him from getting murdered. The only light comes from outside, so I can just discern the silhouette of his body in the bed. He tosses and turns, living through what seems like a horrible nightmare. But there is no attacker.

My heart rate slows as I watch him twitch and squirm. He screams again but not as loud, and I wonder if there were more of these I didn't hear before I woke. I'm sure he's safe now. I should just close the door and go, but I don't. I paint myself an image of a brave girl who would go and sit on his bed, lay a hand on him, and wake him up.

Hell, he fucked me in my sleep. The least he deserves is a little tit for tat, me invading his fitful sleep like he did mine. I want to tell him it's okay and stop the horrible sound of his screams. At least to make myself feel better since my heart can't help aching for him.

Indecision grips me firmly, holding me to the spot. I lost my virginity to him just a few hours ago, and he didn't even cuddle me. I don't know what this is, but it's not some special Christmas romance. Mikhail doesn't want me here.

I walk slowly, closing the door before he can wake and find me there watching him like a creep. Inaction is the worst option of all. Even after I'm outside with that barrier between us, I hear him grunting inside. The scene I just witnessed is more than enough to fuel my imagination of what he looks like as his rigid body squirms. My stupid heart aches, and tears fill my eyes. I can't go back to sleep, not when he's like this. Yet comforting him is out of the question.

The lines between us are blurred, but I know for sure that whatever the deal is, I'm not getting his heart. He's not going to unburden his soul to me and tell me whatever causes him such pain and fear. I'm his ballerina. I'm probably his whore too.

Letting myself believe he's taking me seriously or considering me as a permanent structure in his life is foolish. If I were smart, I would put an end to all of this and guard my part in his production more fiercely. Unfortunately, I'm his whore, and whenever Mikhail looks my way, I give him a little more of myself.

Whether or not he wants me, I belong to Mikhail. I hurt for his pain, live for his approval, and my pussy is desperate for his attention. I'm too far gone.

The apartment around me is proof enough of how different the worlds we come from really are. My mother married into money with Carter, but my father was a simple man. Mikhail makes Carter look like he's middle class. This wealth is generational, obscene, and far outside of something I could be a part of. Maybe I'm his whore, but I'm not the one to hold his hand through his nightmares.

A perfect line draws in front of me. I will never have access to him the way he has it to me, and if I want to enjoy the benefits of this situation, I need to stop fighting that. I need to forget the idea of sitting at his bedside or hoping he's the one who will finally believe me about Carter. It isn't going to happen for me.

I sit there, thinking about myself and what use I am to the people around me. My ear stays pressed to the door, and each time he shouts, my chest aches, and my stomach turns. I stay there on the floor until I don't hear him struggling anymore.

Once it's all peaceful again, I go back to my room. My limbs are heavy as I move, aged by the weight and intensity of his pain. Despite my exhaustion, it takes me a minute to fall asleep with the sounds of his screams dancing in my head.

CHAPTER 15
LYLA
ACT 2

I WOKE up late the following morning. I know I've overslept without looking at a clock just from the angle of the sun. I don't stress for once. It feels good not to have to sneak and pretend, leave the theater and come back in like I'm actually arriving. I'm no longer roommates with the rats or the ghosts, and now that I'm safe and far away in the sky, I feel like I'm in a whole other realm.

What an embarrassing facade it all was, and I'm exceedingly grateful none of the other ballerinas caught me sleeping on the pads. My cheeks burn just at the thought of that level of humiliation, especially after they figured out I was sleeping in my car.

It's snowing again, or it never stopped. I climb out of bed and look out the window, trying to see if any of the snow accumulated on the sidewalks, but I'm too high up, and all I can see are large drifts of it, uninterrupted, sitting on the tops of buildings. I sigh at how dreamy the picture looks.

Taking a quick inventory of the room, I find that while it's sparsely decorated, it lacks nothing that I might need, and everything here is my size. The costumer would have my measurements, so it's not like he had to do anything too crazy to make this happen, but just how long was he planning to bring me here and *why?* I still don't know that, and I find that unsettling enough to put a kink in my otherwise dream morning.

I'm still sore from last night. Having sex for the first time was intense, confusing, not my choice, and I'm left feeling profoundly raw at the lack of intimacy. Then Mikhail's nightmare left me feeling even more scrubbed out. I head into the bathroom where I showered last night, and rather than take another, I opt for a bath. I check the cabinets and grab Epsom salt to soothe the sore flesh between my legs.

After weeks and weeks of cleaning myself over the sink at the gas station, a jetted Jacuzzi tub is my personal miracle. I start the water, making it unbearably hot, pour in a cup of the salt, then step away to undress myself. I look my body over in the mirror as I do. It's hard to see what about me appeals to him, but I suppose I feel fortunate that it does.

Climbing into the tub, I sink my full body up to my chin. I've never been in a tub quite this large, and I moan outright as I turn on the jets and the scalding hot water kneads my muscles. I wash my hair all over again, using up all my shampoo. I want to smell like me again. Clean.

I detangle my hair with my fingers while humming a song. I know I shouldn't be this happy. Whenever I'm happy, something bad strikes, but I need to enjoy it now. Even if all I have is a screaming-hot jetted tub—okay, this is cool.

When I get out, I hit the dresser instead of the closet, which has way more options than I need right now. Choosing a pair of sweats and a baggy T-shirt, I get dressed and leave the bedroom.

His closed door sits slightly down the hall from my own, but I can't imagine he's still in there. Mikhail doesn't strike me as the type to sleep in, and I always see him at the theater early. Memories of his screams last night raise the fine hairs on my arm, and I have to forcibly pull myself away from the scene.

The stairs lead back the way I came last night. I head down, thinking of something less awkward to say when we see each other. The joking thing really didn't work for me, and I don't know if he heard any of my gratitude. Did he leave before I said anything, or did my emotional crap drive him away?

I should be okay with the silence. That's likely what he wants of me too. I've been alone long enough to be okay with that, but when Mikhail is around, I'm a ball of nerves. *I want to talk to him.*

I step out onto the landing, finding that the foyer is actually round with lots of hallways leading off. The large living area with the floor-to-ceiling windows looks a lot different in the daytime. It's still just as white but less stark somehow, almost comfortable, just seriously missing any personal touches.

"Hello?" I whisper at first. "Hello?" I repeat louder when I don't hear anything back.

I circle the living room, looking for him. There are more hallways leading off and down in different directions. You could get seriously lost in this place. I follow one of them down a dark wood-paneled hallway. Finding a set of stairs, I take it to the bottom, where he has a security office. Several cameras are aimed around the apartment, and a view of the foyer sits central. Though it doesn't show all the rooms, it's enough to make me think he's really not home.

It was silly to think we would drive to the theater together, but how else does he expect me to get there? The image of Mikhail driving my piece of shit car here is almost enough to make me laugh. That certainly didn't happen.

Rubbing the space between my brows, I think about how to make the trip from here to the theater in time. It's not exactly close. I don't even know what time it is now, but I refuse to freak out. Worse things have happened to me, after all.

I decide to find the kitchen and look for coffee before I make any decisions. I find the right room as I step through a wide arch, and once again, I gasp. This is seriously beautiful.

He's got a thing for white, and the kitchen is no exception. The stainless steel appliances lining the room shine without a single fingerprint on them. I walk into the room slowly, taking it all in. Much to my surprise, there's a plate on the counter with a note on top. My heart races, thinking about his other notes.

Maybe he noticed I'm practicing. Maybe he knows I'm getting better, and he's proud.

I wish I'd held on to the old ones, but Carter hated them and made a show of throwing each one in the fireplace.

> *Eduard knows you won't be at the theater today.*
> *Eat. Rest.*
> *M.*

Confused, I turn the paper over, expecting him to have said something more, but nothing else is written. From the man who once compared my body to music itself, this particular note falls flat. I smash the feeling and swallow it, resolving to cover it up with the breakfast he left for me.

I don't want to sit around focusing on the past today. While I hate to miss rehearsal, I was just given a chance to rest and eat. Two things I desperately need, and I'm not too proud to ignore the opportunity.

Under the note sits a parcel wrapped in white paper. A delicate circular label with a drawing of a lavender flower that I immediately recognize sticks on the butcher paper. The same bakery the ballerinas always eat from—the ones they keep leaving out...

I unwrap the paper, and it's the same sandwich I've eaten all week. My stomach growls, and I want to dig in, but my mind is working fast.

I step back. I was far too hungry to question the food. Hell, I was okay with stealing it. But I suddenly realize I wasn't stealing it at all. He was feeding me.

I'm divided in my feelings. Part of me is grateful that he helped me when I really needed it, and part of me is profoundly nervous. This mixed with the clothes seems like a little too much. It feels too good to be true, but is any of it real? Ultimately, the answers don't matter because I'm not wasting food and didn't kick up a fuss when he brought me here.

I feel heavy after my food and all these strange revelations, and I end up taking a long nap on one of the couches in the living area.

I don't like that I'm so obedient, especially when I'm concerned he's stocked his home for me like a pet. Still, eating and resting are all I do. There's no sign of Mikhail or anyone else, but food appears on the counter every few hours.

I wonder if this apartment is just as haunted as the theater. Salmon arrives for lunch, and a protein shake appears in the afternoon. I finish them and put the dishes in the sink, and like magic, they're cleaned sometime between meals.

The novelty wears off when it's after eight. Dinner waits for me, but there is still no Mikhail. I eat alone, my stomach bulging. After months of eating scraps, today was an experience. I don't wait around for him. It's obvious he wants to feed me, but I'm not good enough to be around.

I go to sleep in a mood, and I wake up cursing when the same happens. Crossing the hall, I knock on his door, but there's no answer. I set an alarm the night before so I have time to figure out my way to the theater, but Mikhail leaves the same note over my breakfast.

"Fuck you!" I tell the food, but I eat it anyway.

It's delicious, and I hate Mikhail for that, for making everything here so lovely and comfortable but denying me what I want most. After taking my fucking virginity, you wouldn't think something like a little time would be too much to ask for. But I'm an idiot who always seems to forget that expectation breeds disappointment.

I'm not sure what I was thinking when I agreed to come here, but this wasn't it. When I think about it, I didn't exactly *agree* to anything. Mikhail demanded I follow, and I was dumb enough to comply.

I think I hate the man, both for ignoring me and keeping me from the theater.

On day three, I try the lock just to be sure, and of course it's open. I want to kick myself. This is not an abduction. I go down the elevator. The lobby is just as lovely as it was when I arrived. After greeting the doorman, I walk over to the exit to look outside. It's snowy again, the frost on the window telling me it's bitterly cold.

"Miss, I believe you're supposed to be resting."

My brow scrunches as I look back toward the man I've never seen before.

"What?" I'm not sick. I'm actually the healthiest I've been in the past two years.

"Mr. Ivanov wants to ensure you get the rest you need."

I nod, but I wave him away. I'm okay. "I'm much better now, thanks."

I move to the door, and he moves too. He raises his hands as if talking me off the ledge. "Miss, I need you to step away and go rest."

A heavy moment stretches between us, and a creepy feeling blows behind my ear, but I end up agreeing.

"Uh, okay," I tell him as I step away from the door.

I decide to try the common areas. I don't want to be locked up for another second, but my desire to explore the building diminishes as a paranoid suspicion creeps over me. I feel like more than one person is watching me as I walk around. I head back up, wondering if that unlocked door meant anything at all.

The afternoon protein shake is gone in two swallows, and I wipe my mouth with the back of my hand. *I'm bored.*

I don't want to poke around the building where strangers are watching me, and after finding the security office, I'm sure Mikhail could watch me if he was so inclined, but one thing the past few days have taught me is that he's not. Maybe I'm counting on him being able to see me. Perhaps I'm angry that he's left me here after all this time ignoring me.

Walking through the house, I try every door. I throw open the unlocked ones, leaving them for him to find. If he wants to leave me alone so badly, maybe he should see what that looks like.

I've opened about fifteen doors and failed to open about twelve when I come upon one that couldn't be farther from the room he placed me in. I turn the knob, and it fails to twist like it's locked, but the door itself pushes open as if the last person to close it didn't make sure that the latch lined up. The door pushes open, and my mouth drops.

It's all here.

The mirrored wall, the barre, and even a beautiful piano in the corner. I make a beeline for my room, rushing to throw my clothes away and changing into my leotard and tights. I grab my pointes and make a run back to the room, only lacing them up once I'm inside. It's almost like I'm scared to blink, and it's gone. I cue some music on my phone and start to dance, finally free.

The choreography isn't as challenging when I'm not so hungry. I know there's room for improvement, but damn if it doesn't feel nice to throw myself into the rhythm and move my body without the fear I might fall. I'm stronger, and at that moment, I feel unbeatable.

I dance across the room with a passion I forgot existed. I leave everything people have to say about me outside of this building. I forget my own expectations and give in to the magic I've always felt while dancing. I'm free, alive—

"What are you doing?"

I gasp, my pirouette ending so abruptly I almost fall and twist my ankle. Mikhail doesn't seem to care as his eyes laser focus on me. Anger rolls off him as he balls his hands into fists, the air around us thickening.

"I—"

"Leave." The words scraped his throat and cut me up.

I know it hurts him to speak. It must be especially bad after that nightmare the other night. This is the most he has ever said to me, and he's causing himself pain to chase me away.

That stings.

I open and close my mouth, feet rooted to the spot as I try to force my body to respond to my brain.

"LEAVE!" This time, he shouts.

I gasp as his voice cracks and breaks, failing in his throat. Everything comes tumbling down on me. All that I built in the past few days was on his foundation. I have done nothing, repaired nothing. I have nothing.

Before I can run away, the tears come.

Why am I such a miserable fool?

CHAPTER 16
MIKHAIL
ACT 2

MY STUDIO SURROUNDS ME, and though it's not dusty from being abandoned, it feels like a tomb to the old Mikhail. Everything is glossed and perfect, just like it was the last day I closed the door myself.

Part of me wants to go and find my housekeeper to scream some more about the importance of keeping certain rooms locked, but that wouldn't help anyone in this situation, especially given the positive reputation I've managed to maintain with my staff.

I look at everything, images of an old life flashing before my eyes. My jaw aches with an intensity of pain that seems unfair after all this time. We're made to believe modern medicine can fix anything, set right any broken bone, but even with all my money, that's just not true. There is no true escape from the pain.

I'm not even a man as I stand here. I'm a patchwork of my past. I spend my life ignoring what this room meant for me. I no longer compose at my grandfather's piano, for fuck's sake.

A noise of rage and pain echoes from the back of my throat, and my fist snaps out, colliding with one of the walls of glass. Pain shoots up my knuckles, taking the worst of the sting out of my jaw, and a spiderweb fracture forms across the mirror. *God-fucking-dammit.*

The accident took my entire sense of self, a life without constant pain. The young man who danced and composed in this studio may as well have died in that car because he isn't me. It's hard to imagine I was once an eighteen-year-old with dreams that ended at once because of that car crash. The memories were forgotten, abandoned in a fog of my new reality. It feels like pain, and a poorly healed jaw have been my entire life.

This room is proof that Mikhail existed, and she had no business being there. A part of me sees how perfect they would have been for each other—Lyla and that Mikhail I no longer am. The sting in my knuckles worsens, and I look down to find them bruised, bleeding, and decorated with small bits of glass. The old Mikhail certainly wouldn't have done that.

Of course Lyla would find a way to dance even away from the main stage, but I didn't expect her to open every damn door in the place just to piss me off and then wind up here. Since I've brought her home, I've been checking in on her through the cameras, and this is the first time I've had any issue with what I've found.

Maybe I get her frustration to some extent. I'm not sure I'd respond well to the same treatment.

I stare at the floor beneath me, unable to face myself in the now-broken mirror. I'm a fool and too old for this behavior. I know better. My good hand works to pick the larger pieces of glass out of the cuts as I swallow and bury down the feelings coming to the surface.

Emotions are rarely appreciated in high society. From an early age, I learned I would hide them or suffer. It served me well enough all along, but especially when my life came crashing down. I stepped outside of my feelings and became whatever was left of me without them. I had to in order to survive.

But time and time again, the true me comes to the surface, and it's always as a result of Lyla's presence in my life or lack thereof. A feral undercurrent hides under my mannered surface, something primal and unseemly that would humiliate generations of my forefathers if it were to break free. It will only get more intense if I don't possess Lyla the way I need to.

I know I shouldn't be angry, but everything Lyla does drags an intense reaction out of me, and I've worked to avoid any intense reactions. The pain in my knuckles actually helps me to see sense. It's a new pain rather than the one that's tortured me for a decade and a half.

She was practicing the choreography I need her to perform for the upcoming show. I don't dwell on the fact that she should be my prima ballerina if I'm aiming to calm myself. She needs to be perfect to deserve my stage.

She's terribly in need of real food, rest, and a place to stay, but the real reason I've been hiding and avoiding her is because I don't know how to deal with the issue. Carter is all over the theater, the pompous fuckwit. He's trying to pull strings and rank, desperate to establish himself as the top-billed producer there. It won't work.

Pulling myself out of my thoughts, I go to Lyla's room, closing doors along the way. I'm not sure what to say when I get there. My jaw hurts from shouting, which is convenient since I won't apologize anyway. She shouldn't be in that room without permission, but I reacted like a maniac, and she didn't deserve the way I shouted at her.

I bring my hand up to knock, but I remember it's my house, and I don't want to give her a courtesy she didn't extend to me. So I swing the door open. She's sitting on the bed, her legs dangling at the edge. She's so tiny that I feel even worse about my response. She could shatter me emotionally, but physically, I'm so much larger than her. Her eyes narrow at me when I come in, but she's smart enough not to ask me what I'm doing here.

"I'm going to the rehearsal tomorrow," she tells me with her small nose upturned.

I say nothing, working out whatever I want to tell her about my overreaction. She goes where I tell her to go, and I won't argue with her. Lyla doesn't need locked doors to do what she's told, but if I have to impress a point, I will. Lyla jumps from the bed, disturbed once again by the silence. She'll learn to like that, too.

"I have to practice. What will Eduard think? The other ballerinas?"

It doesn't matter what he thinks. He'll do what I tell him to do. The ballerinas are even less of a consideration. I won't entertain their stupid questions either. I stare at her, trying to understand what it is that makes her so fucking irresistible. I can never put my finger on it. She's just some kind of magic.

"I overreacted," I tell her, jaw already screaming in pain from the scene I'm currently trying to make amends for.

"Is that an apology?"

I shake my head. Her gasp of outrage shouldn't travel directly to my cock, but it does.

"I don't know why you have a room people aren't allowed in. It's stupid."

This earns her an arched brow. I have many rooms people aren't allowed in. This was just the only one that happened to be left open. She's pissed and trying to push me just like she was with those doors. I can't deny that the lack of my attention seems to have made an impression on her. After years of being obsessed with her, it's rather gratifying to watch her yearn for me.

I stare her down, waiting for her next stupid argument, wondering if maybe I should say more. She starts to fidget under the weight of my gaze. That's when she notices my hand. I wasn't hiding it from her, but I wasn't waving it around either. I'm not proud of myself.

"Mikhail, what the hell happened?" she gasps, surprising me with the genuine concern in her voice.

I don't answer but just watch in shock as she runs to my side and grabs my hand. She lifts it gently, careful not to hurt me, and holds it up to her face to look.

"Your knuckles are full of glass," she speaks matter-of-factly, but her lip trembles. I try to pull my hand out of hers before she gets any of my blood on her. "Let me clean them," she insists, and I pull my hand more forcefully this time.

"No," I tell her sternly, and the most lovely look of disappointment warps her expression.

"How did this happen?" she asks, but I have absolutely no intention of telling her. If I have things my way, she'll never see the mirror anyway, but my cheeks warm, and I can't help but be embarrassed.

"You didn't!" she accuses me, hands slapping against my chest. "You didn't hurt the studio!"

I did, in fact, hurt the studio, so I'm not sure how to respond. She brushes a strand of hair out of her face, her big brown eyes aimed at me as if she knows I think about her day and night.

"This was incredibly stupid," she tells me, lightly lifting my hand again.

I nod. There isn't a chance in hell I would try to deny what's so obvious.

"Everyone acts impulsively sometimes." It almost sounds like she's speaking to herself as she examines me. "Let me help you get this clean and wrapped, and then we'll clean up the studio too if it needs it."

I shake my head again, and my face warps with my displeasure at not being listened to. She's not cleaning my fucking hand when I deserve what I get for punching my own shit.

"Mikhail, I don't understand. Why won't you let me take care of you when you so clearly need it?" She slaps her hands on her hips like I am the most confounding creature in existence and not the other way around.

"You're the one who clearly needs to be taken care of." I aim a sharp look at her. The ways I want to punish her for living so dangerously number in the thousands.

I still haven't figured out just how long she was homeless, but the fact she was makes me insane. Especially when I could have made it right for her so easily. I want to smack her ass black and blue for choosing the cold when I was an option, and I don't care if that feeling is unreasonable. She should have known I'd always want her.

"Come on, you've taken care of me for days. Let me return the favor." There's really only one way I want her to take care of me, and if there are knuckles involved, they'll be inside her.

I stare in complete astonishment as she lifts my hand again, but this time, she presses a kiss to one of my knuckles, smearing my blood on her top lip.

Fuck.

CHAPTER 17
MIKHAIL
ACT 2

"STOP, YOU'LL HURT YOURSELF." I pull my hand back again, but she steps forward with it.

We're incredibly close now. Her perfume is sweet, her lashes long and dark in contrast with her pale blond hair. She's small, but sometimes she can undo me with just a look. I've wanted this closeness with her since I took her for myself in the dressing room, but I admit a part of me was afraid if I'd asked, she wouldn't have said yes. Lyla surprises me, though. I thought she was mine, so I took what belonged to me. Now I think she might agree with me.

I reach her chin with my fingers, feeling her soft skin against mine. If she wants to take care of me so badly, I have a way. My cock presses against my zipper, and I watch that pouty mouth, wondering how sweet her trepidatious sucks would be.

No one's ever had her mouth. Her pussy was practically a religious experience. I don't care if it's sick—her inexperience thrills me. I bet she doesn't know how to suck a cock, but the Lyla I know is an eager student.

"Suck me," I tell her as I push my thumb over her fat bottom lip. Her pink tongue comes out to taste me, and I groan. My blood smears farther, the pain in my hand all but forgotten, and the gruesome sight of her with my blood on her face brings that savage creature I try to hide barreling to the surface.

Her eyes light up like it's fucking Christmas. Words won't show her who I am. Since the accident, I have stopped relying on them. Words aren't worth much. People lie and say things they don't mean. I don't waste my time putting my thoughts into words. I put them into action instead.

My thumb pushes inside her mouth, and she sucks it with an eagerness that echoes straight down my cock, humming while she does it. My whole body tenses. I need her too much, and there are too many intense emotions fueling that lust. I'm blinded any time she's in the room. I can't see anything but her and how I can use her to sate my desires.

I pull my thumb from her mouth, squishing her bottom lip roughly between my fingers, revealing her bottom teeth and making her whimper. She doesn't protest, and I let her go, switching to holding her chin between my fingers with just a little too much force.

She's so pretty. So delicate. I close my hand around her neck and squeeze just enough to prevent her from speaking. She can breathe with a little effort. She tries, and her throat rasps from her attempt. Alarm lights her brown eyes as she stares at me, but it switches to hunger as I nudge her down to her knees.

She kneels in front of me, blond hair cascading around her face. My fingers flex against her throat. It's not a threat but an insistence on my ownership. She's mine and looks so pretty with my hand around her throat. Her eyes are on me, waiting for what comes next, and that hint of her fear dies to her excitement.

I've dreamed of seeing Lyla in this position a thousand times. I know that each time, each way I fuck her, I'll be just as ruined as the first time. I should think twice about sinking deeper into my obsession with her. I already plan to keep her no matter what she wants. Wrapping myself more tightly around her finger is a bad plan.

But that's exactly what I do as I pull my pants open and let my cock fall free. My erection bounces in front of her face, and my good little slut licks her lips in anticipation.

I grip the base, squeezing hard and taking the worst of the edge off, though my precum is leaking. My heart hammers inside my chest at the sight of her. Lyla licks her lips, and a small crease forms between her brows. I smear the head of my cock over her lips, spreading it on her. She flicks her tongue again, tasting me.

"I've never done this before. You'll have to teach me what you like."

Oh, that's exactly what I intend to do. Electricity runs through my whole body. My deepest desire was always to teach my little ballerina to perform like I want. To show her and the world what her body can do.

"Open," I tell her, and she obeys, making room for the head of my cock to swipe against her tongue. "Suck."

She's so fucking good. She closes her mouth around me and applies the most divine suction. I know I should be gentle with her and teach her like she asked. This is her first time doing this, after all, but the animal she draws out of me is poised at the surface, and gentile Mikhail is nowhere to be found.

I wind my fist into her hair, hissing when I remember the cuts and glass in the knuckles of my dominant hand, but too late now, I'm fucking her mouth. She makes a noise of shock and overwhelm as I drag her forward, throwing off her center of balance and hitting the back of her throat with my cock.

This isn't an apology, but I already admitted I wasn't sorry, and I need to use her to work off this fucking rage. She's my ballerina; she's my pretty little fuck toy, mine to use. The tension in her throat eases after a minute, and her eyes open to meet mine, staring at me through the rough, wet thrusts.

She takes me so deep, and she's not even gagging anymore. Her throat is so fucking tight. My jaw locks with the pressure of clenching it, but the pleasure is so intense I don't feel the worst of it. I finally slow the pace, holding her hair just as firmly and using her for my pleasure. I give her the time to really suck and roll her tongue around me, and shit, is she doing an amazing job of it.

I grunt, my hips surging as I fuck her mouth. I pull her to the edge and legitimately moan when she sucks all the way to the tip and pops off with a wet snap. She moans like a little slut as she takes me back into her mouth, but I stop her with the hand in her hair.

Patience, I tell her with my eyes, watching as she grinds her thighs together. She whines low in her throat, and fuck, I'm not patient either. I slam back inside her, eyes rolling to the back of my head as she sucks me down. Her eyes beg me to let go, to let her suck at the pace she wants, but she's already taken too much and invaded too much of my space. I'm going to come down her throat exactly when and how *I* want to.

Her hair is soft between my fingers, but it stings against my self-inflicted injuries. I'm a fucking asshole, but it's worth it if I get to feel her hot mouth around my cock. Her perfume is everywhere in this room, and I'm barely able to remember my name as my orgasm starts to build and my balls draw up. A tingle starts at the base of my spine, and before I know it, I spill for her.

Thick ropes of cum spill into her mouth, so much she gags to swallow me. I could be kind, back off, and give her room to breathe and adjust to the new experience of hot cum in her throat, but I don't. I use my hold on her hair to push myself so deep, she has to gag as she swallows me.

Tears form on her lashes as she does, and no matter how

hard it is for her to take, she doesn't fight me. Tears drip from the corner of her eyes, and a stray pearl of cum seeps from the corner of her battered lips.

She looks gorgeous. So fucking perfect.

Holding myself for a count of three, I eventually pull my hips back and free her throat, enjoying the drag of her lips over my cock. Leaving myself coated in her spit and dripping one last bead of cum, I tuck myself back inside my pants. My hand moves to her soft cheeks.

"You're such a good girl for me, Lyla."

She pants, staring up at me like I have everything she needs.

"Fuck me, please."

I just give her a long look. If she wants my cock that bad, she'll be easier to mold. I want to fuck her more than anything, but I know better than just to give her what she wants. Just like in my production, if she wants my cock, she needs to earn it.

"No," I say without leaving any room for arguments. I turn and head for the door, but right before I'm gone, I tell her over my shoulder, "And don't touch yourself."

I leave her in her room to squirm, feeling the first shreds of control I have all day.

CHAPTER 18
LYLA
ACT 2

MY EYES open at exactly six in the morning, my natural sleep pattern returning now that I can eat and sleep with shelter. I don't even bother getting properly dressed before I head across the hall and knock on his door.

No answer. *There's no way I missed him again.* Running downstairs to yell at him, I'm wearing only a loose T-shirt and arrive in the kitchen thinking there's no way I could have missed him, but he's not there.

"Dammit!" I slap my hands against my hips before realizing my dower director might not be here, but someone else is.

Graying curls frame her face, and there's just enough lines in her skin for me to notice. My cheeks burn at my language and my ass hanging out. This is the first time I've seen anyone else in the apartment, but I wonder if I simply haven't been getting up early enough.

"Good morning."

"Hi..." I smile awkwardly as I try to pull the hem of my shirt down.

My toes curl against the wooden floor. All I want is to run back to my room, get dressed, and then find a way to yell at

Mikhail. Obviously, I can't. He's too intense for that, but the desire only grows with my humiliation.

"Sit down, dear. Have your breakfast. It just got delivered. Still hot."

The wrapped food is once again waiting for me, and my eyes narrow at the parcel. I obviously love being fed, and my growling stomach is a giveaway, but I'm annoyed that he keeps sneaking out without me. And I'm even more annoyed that I don't confront him or even hop on a bus and just leave. Would the doorman really do anything if I did? He'd definitely tattle, I decide.

"I'll just be right back," I tell her, getting ready to head back to my room and grab my pants.

"Don't fuss, dear. It's nothing I haven't seen before."

A jealous part of me worries very much she means specifically with Mikhail. Does she mean she saw other women here?

I could argue, but I'm going to be sitting on my ass anyway, so I take my place at the table. Sure, food and rest were necessary at first, but I'm going insane now. I need to get back to the theater. The first show is quickly approaching, and I'm getting nervous that I'll ruin the whole thing without real practice with the cast. I don't like to deliver anything but my absolute best.

Taking a deep breath, I sit at the table. I go to open the breakfast, but before I get the chance, the woman snatches it up. She disappears into the kitchen to return a moment later with it nicely served on a plate. I salivate when I see pancakes coming my way with a healthy portion of berries on the side.

"Oh, I love pancakes," I tell her as she places them in front of me. Grabbing the fork and knife, I start to dig in, expecting something comforting and familiar. My smile falls off my face as I realize these aren't the usual fluffy and sweet pancakes of my childhood. I chew the dry cake, coughing a little.

A cake is a generous term for this, and there's not even the mercy of syrup to soften it up. It's not exactly bad, and nothing about it tastes unpleasant. But surely, it should have a different name and shape so as not to trick hungry, angry ballerinas. The woman chuckles at my expression and makes a show of reading the receipt attached to the wrapping.

"Protein-loaded pancakes."

"Of course." I roll my eyes, but I keep eating. There's no way in hell I'll discard good food just because it's not so good. When you're truly hungry, you learn not to waste food.

By the third mouthful, I'm liking it more and more. It's kind of like a dry, bready oatmeal in flavor. The berries really make it decent, and I polish off the entire thing.

"I'm Molly, by the way." She introduces herself."

I wince, covering my mouth with one hand and offering her the other to shake. "I'm so sorry. I got distracted by the food."

"Don't worry. Mikhail told me to make sure you eat, but I don't think that's a problem."

My cheeks turn bright red, and she immediately apologizes, but I wave her off. It's not her fault I'm especially sensitive about food.

"So he insisted I eat, but he left for the theater without me again?"

Brown eyes crinkle at the edges as she narrows them. Molly seems kind enough, but she knows too much.

"He didn't actually say anything about you eating this morning specifically. That's an ongoing complaint of his." She smiles, and I clear my throat to concentrate on my empty plate.

"Do you work for Mr. Ivanov, or is this a favor?"

It's a silly attempt to generate conversation, but I'm also starved for any information on Mikhail.

"That's complicated, but we'll call this a favor."

"Hmm." I nod.

That's not much of an answer, and I find that after being

locked up here all these days, I'm not in the mood for riddles. I'm less irritated with my full belly, and I guess if this is a favor, I should at the very least say thanks.

"I appreciate it."

She smiles. "No problem."

I want to ask her more questions, like what the hell does *it's complicated* mean. Before I can fire them off, the intercom buzzes, and Molly goes to answer with an ease and familiarity I envy.

When she returns, I'm still in the same place, and she doesn't volunteer who it was. I guess she has no reason to, but it still feels rude.

It's tiring trying to figure out what is happening here. I rub my temple, already getting a headache from trying to understand this man. The hot-and-cold routine is getting on my nerves today. He knows I need to practice, yet he won't bring me to the theater or let me in his studio here. Molly must notice I'm out of it because she watches me carefully before nodding to herself.

"I have to grab a few things at the store. Do you want to come with me?" She offers me a lifeline I have no intention of denying.

"Yes, please. Let me get dressed," I say quickly before she changes her mind.

She laughs at my eagerness, but I don't care. I dart up the stairs to do exactly that. If I wasn't so bored and starved for company, I'd be more embarrassed by how ready I am to spend time with a stranger, but it's really more of a chance at freedom. I'm rested now. I'm done staying hidden away up here.

I head to the closet because the clothes in the dresser aren't warm enough, and I'm overwhelmed by how much stuff is in here. I've been trying to avoid it, as realizing just how much planning Mikhail put into bringing me here sends a little chill running up my spine.

I pick out a beautiful pair of lined leggings and a rose-colored sweatshirt. I grab a hat and a thick coat, and a pair of boots. Pulling everything on, I hold a pair of gloves I'm not sure I'll wear. I quickly check myself in the mirror and decide I look cute with my blond hair spilling from beneath the hat and over my shoulders.

"That was fast," she tells me as I press the button, and we take the elevator to the lobby.

The doorman watches us carefully as we leave. Rather than ignoring him or even greeting him, she gives him a stern look. He nods in response. *Huh.*

She notices my attention on their interaction and grabs me by the elbow to lead me into the street.

"Let's grab some fresh produce," she says as she pulls me into a gust of cold December wind. I breathe deep, the pain in my lungs proving just how cold it is today. My hands slip into the gloves I wasn't sure I'd need, and I'm grateful for their warmth.

Molly leads the way, taking me through the nicest neighborhood I've ever been in. Old buildings line the street with columns and arches, elaborate filigree in stone, and not a speck of graffiti to be seen. Eventually, we stop at a small corner shop a couple of blocks away.

She pushes the door open ahead of us, and a bell jingles merrily overhead. Soft, jazzy, and warm Christmas music plays on the radio. A tower of wine bottles in an elaborate display that looks like a Christmas tree allows you to take bottles off the racks in front. Chocolate bars, cards, and anything else that might serve as a good Christmas present have been pushed toward the front of the store for the last-minute shopper heading to a Christmas party.

Rows and piles of carefully labeled organic fruits and vegetables line the wall and form their own small section to the right. The colors are too beautiful to be real. One particular cauliflower is green and covered in fractal patterns like a snowflake or a Christmas bauble. *Romanesco,* the little sign reads. There are multiple other fruits and vegetables I've never seen before. Molly picks up a few things and puts them into her basket.

My mouth hangs open when she takes me to the shelves with freshly baked sourdough bread, which smells the same as the sandwiches I found in the dressing room. This is the fancy bakery he gets my food from every day. The counter at the back has all the most beautiful sandwiches and pastries, and it leads to a small kitchen. I grab the menu, noticing none of the items he ordered for me are listed.

"Good morning, Evelyn." Molly sneaks past me to address the woman at the counter.

They talk briefly, and Molly grabs a good selection of bread and cheese. It looks like they know each other. Molly must shop here frequently—my stomach sinks. *She* is probably the one coming here for my food, not Mikhail.

I wish more than anything his lack of attention didn't feel like a punch to the gut, but it does. Being so upset about this is stupid, but I am. I've told myself again and again to stop making myself the victim of my own unmet expectations, and here I am, placing them time and time again on Mikhail. It was silly to imagine a man like him, with all manner of commitments, would find the time in his day to do that for me. He likely doesn't have the time to do it for himself.

Still, I liked the fantasy of Mikhail spending his time as well as his money and effort on choosing something just for me. He's such a serious man. I imagined him waffling over which dish would be the best for me, and that small act felt more intimate than it should have been.

I manage to swallow my snort when Molly introduces me to Evelyn as Mikhail's friend.

"I'm one of his ballerinas," I say to Evelyn, pretty sure friends are acknowledged and not fucked while sleeping on stunt pads.

The next half an hour or so, Molly leads me around the store, helping me pick out things I want. I'm initially uncomfortable as I certainly don't have the money to shop here, but she talks me into it. We both buy a lot at the corner store, but nothing leaves with us. They'll be delivered later today. We head back to the building, and I'm sad to say goodbye to this faux freedom.

"Molly, this arrived for Mr. Ivanov." The doorman rushes to show us a package when we finally return.

The box is fairly large but doesn't look heavy. I offer to take it for Molly anyway. She thanks him, and we go back up in the elevator. My eyes trace the label as the car moves upward. It's from a pharmacy, and I can only assume it's medicine. How strange.

The elevator doors open, letting us out into Mikhail's apartment, and I place the box on the table. Her phone chimes, and she smiles, satisfied with whatever she sees. "Our shopping will be here by four."

"I can put everything away," I offer. "You don't need to stay around." I don't make a snarky comment about working for Mikhail being complicated, but I want to.

Molly waves me away. "One of us will handle everything. We're around, don't worry."

Part of me wants to ask who "we" is, but I settle on the curiosity that unsettles me more. "Where?"

She looks me over, eyes scrutinizing like she's working very hard to figure out a hidden meaning in my question. She crosses her arms over her chest. "I live in the building. Fifth floor. James downstairs will probably call me when everything arrives."

"Oh. I didn't know." I nod, trying to make sense out of things. This is a crazy expensive building to live in, and something doesn't make sense. Why is her employment status complicated, and what does it have to do with her being able to afford all this?

"Mikhail owns the building," she tells me, momentarily knocking the air out of my lungs. "Ivanov is his father's name, but his mother was… Well, you can see her name on the building." She smiles smugly like Mikhail's points of pride somehow belong to her too. "He makes sure the people loyal to him are taken care of."

For once, I'm stunned into complete silence. He owns one of the most iconic buildings in this city?

Wow.

"It's a gorgeous place to live." My smile is forced, but Molly doesn't say anything as she watches my pained expression.

"Well, I'll be going now," she says, and I just nod. Of course she had to, and I'm even more of a fool to be disappointed that this near stranger won't spend her entire day with me.

I brush my hair out of my face, and then I remember. "Oh, and thank you for everything. For the food and all since I got here."

Molly laughs, shaking her head. "Oh no. That was all Mikhail. I've been visiting my daughter for the past two weeks. She just gave me another grandson."

"Congratulations," I manage to say automatically, but I'm only more confused. "Wait. So Mikhail was picking up food for me?"

"Yes, as far as I know. I told you our working relationship is complicated. I suppose he could have asked someone else, but he didn't ask me."

I rub my face. That's not really an answer either. Once again, I'm overwhelmingly confused about who the man I now live with is. I sit down on the couch about ready to sob, and I don't bother hiding it from Molly. I'm so tired of hiding my emotions.

"Are you okay, Lyla?"

I crane my neck to look at her. I want to say yes, but the lie never comes. "No."

"Tell me what's wrong."

I shake my head. "I don't get him, and I'm not sure if my being here is making any difference to him at all."

Feeling like a fool, I stop myself from saying anything more. I have no reason to believe that she and I are speaking in confidence.

"Do you know what happened to him? Why he needs that?" She nods toward the box of medicine.

I shake my head.

"He was in a car accident when he was young. The hit was ugly, and he had extensive damage to his skull and jaw. He's lucky he didn't have permanent brain damage. He couldn't talk for a year, and even now, those joints don't move right.

"He's always in pain, and that makes a man tired, but it's not only the pain. He learned to live his life with very few words, so he's not used to expressing himself. Sometimes we need to judge him by his actions and assume the best of him."

"What if his actions are just as confusing as his lack of explanations?"

She smiles at me. "Then maybe you need to pay better attention."

CHAPTER 19
LYLA
ACT 2

HIS SCREAMS PENETRATE MY DREAMS, his despair dragging me out by my throat. I gasp, but this time, I'm not confused. *Mikhail is having a nightmare about his accident.*

My eyes fill with tears as I think about what all that means. His pain, his silence. How many nights has he spent alone screaming just like this?

Once again, I can't stop myself. Climbing out of bed, I grab a robe. Frost clings to the window, and there's a chill in the air like the heat got turned down or someone left a window open.

I head down the hall, stopping only for a moment in front of his door. I touch the wood as if it's going to give me the permission I seek, but Molly's advice rings inside my head.

He can't ask.

I wait another moment, trying to decide, but another shout makes my decision for me, and I go in.

The scene is similar to the other night, but I don't plan on leaving like I'm helpless this time. His body tosses and turns, straining against his memories, and I admit I wait a few moments too long as I wrestle with my nerves. This time, I do what I should have done before and close the door behind me.

The possibility of his rejection shoots anxiety and sparks of adrenaline through my system as I cross the room. This one impulsive action might screw up what little we've managed to build, but that doesn't stop me.

"Mikhail?" I call softly as I sit on the edge of the bed. He must have taken a similar position that night on the stunt pads. My whole body warms slightly at the memory.

His pain shakes me. Is this how he feels all the time? Is he simply better at hiding it during the day when he's less raw and exposed, or does all of this wait for him at night?

His warm sheets smell like him. My fingers graze the back of his hand, thinking that simple act is enough to wake him, but nothing happens. Crazy thoughts of fucking him like he did to me cross my mind, and maybe I'll do exactly that another day, when he's dreaming pleasant things. Lifting my leg up and over him, I kneel on the bed and lean a little of my weight against him.

He still doesn't respond to the pressure, but he doesn't throw me off, and I take that as a win. His back presses flat against the mattress, his movements jerky. A grunt tears from his throat, and his pain kills me. *I can't take it anymore.* Making a split-second decision, I lay my body flat over his.

"It's all a dream, Mikhail," I whisper.

Our chests press together, legs tangling, and my mouth poised a breath away from his. His movements stop suddenly. Tension tightens his every muscle, so I smooth my hand over his hair, carefully brushing it out of his face. His silky hair slips between my fingers, reminding me of the forever soft ribbons on my pointe. I have to swallow my giggle and the urge to ask what shampoo he uses.

"It's okay," I tell him, resting my head on his chest.

He's warm and hard in all the right ways. Listening to his breathing and heart slowing, I close my eyes to rest with him, just like I wanted that first night he took my virginity. His breathing changes, and his tense muscles relax, so I know he's awake. He doesn't say anything for a long few moments.

"Lyla," he breathes.

"You were screaming," I tell him. "I'm sorry I came in. I just couldn't handle—"

His arms squeeze me, keeping me in place, and I bury my nose into his neck. Mikhail doesn't talk about his nightmare, but he doesn't let me go for a second. The silence stretches between us as I listen to his heartbeat and trace patterns up and down his arm. I'm starting not to mind the silence the way I did before, but maybe it's time for him to get used to sharing too.

"These cookies my mom used to bake were my favorite thing about Christmas," I say to the silence. "She loved the holidays, you know? Even after my dad died, maybe especially after my dad died. She wanted something really good for us to look forward to." I wait a moment to continue, but his head is tipped in my direction, so I'm satisfied he's listening.

"She always took me to this department store and bought us the prettiest outfits. We have tons of professional pictures of us in these silly, over-the-top outfits."

I swallow hard before I continue. The time after Dad died and before Carter was heart-wrenching and full of grief but sweet in many ways too. My mother tried so damn hard for me.

"She had this necklace, and I don't even know why, but I thought it was the most beautiful thing I had ever seen. It was a teardrop gold pendant with a ruby right in the middle.

"One Christmas, the clasp broke, but it was her special Christmas necklace, and she wasn't going to wait for a store to open it, so she pulled a red velvet ribbon off one of the gifts and wore it. I was seven. I remember looking at that necklace and thinking my mother is the most beautiful woman in the world."

Tears fill my eyes even though I didn't plan to get emotional. I miss my mother and father so badly, but this story was just meant as a distraction, a Christmas story.

"Anyway." I brush it off. "Carter has all of her things. A lot of mine too..."

I search for something else to say, but it's hard to walk away from it now that I've mentioned Carter's name. I'm still thinking about it when Mikhail shifts, moving my body from on top of him to beside him. Even with the low light, his eyes devour me.

He grabs my chin between his fingers and closes the space between us. For a second, I think he's going to kiss me, but he doesn't. We breathe into the empty space, the tension building deliciously between us.

Our chemistry is like magic. My thoughts focus on him alone. His warm hands shift from my chin to my neck and down my chest. He pushes my robe open, groaning when he sees I decided to sleep in one of the fine silk nightgowns.

He takes my breast into his palm, teasing my nipple with those skilled fingers through the fine fabric. Somehow it's even warmer than his bare touch. I sigh in a mix of relief and building anticipation for what he'll do next. How can he dominate all my thoughts so easily?

He slowly pushes my robe off my shoulders, plucking the straps of my nightgown and pulling them down my oversensitive skin. I want him to take me like he did our first time on those stunt pads. Every inch of me vibrates, practically begging him to rush.

The sun is just beginning to crack the horizon in the distance, but Mikhail doesn't give in to my impatient desires as he makes it his mission to touch and taste every part of me except where I want him most. He's pure torment as lips, hands, and teeth search, tease, and punish my body, picking out the ticklish spots. He's playing me like I'm his piano, and all he wants is to see me break.

Flames rush my body, my back arches, and my pussy aches, desperate for him to take me again. His voice grates as he whispers into my ear, still rough from the screams.

"Touch your pussy."

My eyes roll back, and my hand slips between my legs before he finishes the sentence. I dip two fingers inside myself, appreciating just how badly I want him. Using my dripping fingers, I apply pressure to my clit. In half a second, I'm already gasping.

His demands are everything. They shape my body while I dance and control the food going into my mouth. He snaps his fingers, and I'm wet.

As I move faster, the pleasure only grows. A sharp grip pulls my eager fingers away, and I whine at the loss of sensation. My eyes find his, revealing my confusion. My complaint sits on the tip of my tongue when Mikhail forces my hand to his mouth and closes his lips around my fingers.

A chill runs down my spine when I *feel* his jaw fight not to open, but I hide my reaction. It's not disgust but horror at his pain.

Carefully, he pulls my fingers to the back of his throat, and I shiver as his tongue laps them. He groans, the vibration surprisingly pleasurable as it travels up my hand.

"Don't hurt yourself," I tell him, but I know it's too late to avoid it entirely.

"I don't care."

I pull my fingers back, but he bites. "Shit! Ow. I do care about hurting *you*."

He raises a mischievous eyebrow at me.

"Give me more, or I'll hurt myself worse trying to get my tongue in your cunt."

Well, I can't have that, can I? The same two fingers pump slowly into my pussy, as my other hand teases my clit. My toes curl, my desire to come warring with my desire to please and obey him. Of course his approval wins out, and I take my fingers and spread my juices over his lips.

He nips my fingers again as he pulls them deep into his mouth.

He groans as he tastes me again, and I'm filled with a rush of power at being the one to draw this reaction out of Mikhail Ivanov. That intensity lurking beneath his calm facade is what intrigues me most about him, that and how fucking good he makes me feel.

He keeps his teeth tight around my fingers as he slips one of his own inside my pussy. It's so much thicker than my own that one takes up just as much space.

"Oh god," I moan low in my throat as he adds another finger. I'm still so inexperienced. All of these things are new and intense. Wrestling with my impending climax, I try to hold out as long as I can.

"I have to come," I whine.

"Make a mess for me."

He presses his fingers to my G-spot, changing the angle enough to make me feel profoundly full, like I'm about to pee.

He drops down on the bed beside me, removing his fingers just long enough to grip my thighs and pull me up and over his face. I cry at the loss and the sudden change in position, but soon, his fingers are back inside me.

"Oh god, please don't." This is so much more embarrassing than I ever imagined, but he's staring at me with pure hunger and reverence. He's perhaps more desperate to taste me than I am to come.

His look is familiar like he does when I dance, an intensity that I've never seen from anyone.

"Touch your clit. Show me what you like."

He watches the movements of my fingers in silence, marching his fingers to my pace. His expression says this is the best ballet he's ever witnessed, and he's desperate for the finale—I am too. His attention brings me to a new level, and I can't even remember being embarrassed as I let go, coming as I shout his name.

Wet heat pours from between my legs, splashing his hands and face, dropping down my thighs and coating me. Jesus, when Mikhail comes, it's nowhere near this big of a mess.

My orgasm runs past my knees, soaking the bed. It pools in the divots my knees make and wets the tips of his black hair. My head spins, and I feel wrung out like a sponge and in need of water.

I look down at my director with an apology on my lips, but I find him with the most serene expression. *I squirted in his face*, yet Mikhail looks the closest I've ever seen him to happy.

"Delicious," he tells me as he pulls his cock out of his pants.

CHAPTER 20
MIKHAIL
ACT 2

IF I STOP for too long and think about what this really means, I won't do it. It's time, and she needs a place to practice. I turn the knob and open the door of the old studio, averting my eyes so I don't need to deal with what this place means or the damn crack in the glass.

I make a point of leaving the door completely open. I want her to see and understand this is not a mistake.

It's an invitation.

She needs to practice, and I'm not ready to share her with the world just yet. She's in my house, eating what I provide. When I get home, I can enjoy a lungful of her perfume, and yesterday, her wet pussy stained my sheets. I'm not ready to share that with anyone.

More than just my possessive feelings over my little ballerina, her stepfather is still in the theater. His mediocre production ends today, so the stage will be all ours again tomorrow. I'll breathe easier when he's not around anymore.

I've been avoiding the bastard this whole week. It's not good for business if I kill him backstage, and that's what'll happen if our paths cross.

He touched her. He destroyed her trust. He made her fucking homeless.

I've already decided he'll need to be dealt with, but I'm not sure how to pull that off just yet, so I keep her away and avoid him at all costs.

He'll pay for what he did, but helping Lyla will be a lot more difficult in prison.

If I thought I was obsessed before, it's nothing compared to now. No one has ever seen me the way she has or comforted me through my nightmares... I'm too far gone now. There's no way I'll ever let her leave me.

Lyla still sleeps in my bed, the oversized T-shirt she wears all tangled up and showcasing her perfect little tits. Leaving was torture, and even now, each step I take away from her is just a little too tough.

But I have work to do today, and so does she. We have our first show in a couple of days, and I don't tolerate mediocrity. All of my ballerinas need to perfectly meet the expectations set upon them.

By the time I make it to the foyer, her breakfast is being delivered. I tip the driver right when Molly comes down and grabs the parcel for me.

"Are you keeping her in again?" she asks.

I arch an eyebrow, and it's all the answer she needs. Molly shakes her head, giving me an affectionate pat on my arm. "She's not a toy for you to refuse to share."

She raised me when my own parents weren't interested in the job, so I nod respectfully even though she's wrong. Lyla is mine to keep and play with. I don't want to share her with the rest of the world, and now that she's here, I don't need to share with anyone.

My car arrives just in time, and I dip my chin to Molly before getting in. I avoid looking her way. She doesn't fully know how it feels for me to be inside a car, but she has an idea, and I don't like that.

As soon as I sit down, the leather smell triggers me, and as the car rolls forward, my vision closes like curtains after a show. My leg bounces in an attempt to release nervous energy, and my jaw ticks painfully. *Goddammit, maybe I should just quit and take the subway.*

The pain isn't just because of the car ride. Since Lyla entered my life, I'm speaking much more than I should. The recommendation is not at all. I can't eat solid food, for Christ's sake, and eventually, I won't be able to avoid Lyla at meal times. What will she think of a man limited to blended soups and smoothies? *What a life.*

My pride withers.

Lyla is different. I want her to understand my demands. I want her to know what I want and how I want it so I can sit back and watch while she moves mountains to do it. To make herself perfect for me because I will never be perfect for myself.

I arrive at the theater, and Eduard talks them through the stage and costume rehearsal. Lyla is supposed to be with them, but a gap between dancers marks her place. I sit at the back, watching them move. My fingertips drum over my leg as the notes ascend.

My prima ballerina enters the room, and she's gushing about her costume. It's bright and swallows her figure. She goes over her routine, and I'm bored before she's even finished. She's technically adequate, but something is missing when she dances. I need connection and for her to understand the music, but all she's doing is the choreography.

It's lifeless.

And I blame Lyla. She was supposed to be the one up there. She's perfect for the role, yet I won't cast her just based on the memory of who she used to be. She has yet to earn a place in this company. My eyes follow the rehearsal for a little longer, but I'm done for today. I send a message to Eduard reminding him to put Lyla's costume to the side, then I head to my office and bury my nose in paperwork.

I'm in a bad mood, and I can't hide. I need commitment and perfection from all my dancers. Nothing else will do. We are days away from opening our doors, and I don't feel any of them is truly ready to perform at the level I expect. I'm consumed by my thoughts when I enter the office and find a small package waiting for me on the desk. A simple wrapping with an extravagant bow. I watch it from a distance. No one who knows me would send me a gift.

Well, Lyla would.

Lyla is the only person in this world naive enough to try to warm my cold heart. I don't understand why she'd send the gift here when I see her at home every day, but I take the parcel and open it while sitting back in my chair.

Brown leather gloves.

Simple and basic, and I must admit I'm a little disappointed in her. Why would she spend money she doesn't have on something that I have at least two identical pairs?

A note rests on the bottom, and I wonder if she at least explained herself.

Thank you for making me your ballerina.
Love,
Judith.

Who the fuck is Judith?

I spend only a half second trying to remember since I never memorize any of their names. Picking up my paperwork, I go down the list until I find Judith. She's the prima ballerina, of course. The one I wasn't so impressed by.

I throw the useless gloves in the trash right with her note. It rubs me the wrong way that she called herself my ballerina. Sure, they are all dancers for my company this Christmas, but only one of those dancers is mine in any way that matters.

And it's not her.

She's not the one who moves like music itself. She's not the one I can't stop thinking about. She's not the one who I guard so close that I'm filled with pride because I managed to lure her into my home without any fuss.

She's not my ballerina.

The hours tick away, but I do very little work. I look at the costume I laid on the chair, and I can't stop myself from imagining her in it. Ultimately, my desires win, and I take the hanger with the costume and rush home, planning to bring her into my room to try it on.

Music hits me the moment I step inside, but it stops abruptly and restarts. The same thing happens again, and this time, the not so delicate sound of her curse follows. Both are clear signs she's not getting the choreography right. As I climb the stairs, she marks each of her frustrations with a curse. Her little mouth is filthy when she thinks she's alone.

Bringing her costume to my room, I let her do her own thing for now. My suit jacket lands on the bed, and I roll my sleeves up. I perk up when the music goes for a second longer than before, thinking she finally got it, but then her frustrated scream echoes around the house, and the music restarts.

I think I've had enough of letting her figure things out on her own with her filthy mouth. She seems to only be frustrating herself more. I grab the costume and head down the hall, telling myself I'm a very well-intentioned man. I stop in front of the studio's open door, hungry, eager to force greatness out of her and myself into her.

Lyla stands in the middle of the room, her face red from exhaustion, tendrils of hair falling from her bun and whipping around as she practices Fouetté turns. She balances on one leg, the other whipping around her at an impressive speed. She seems to be getting it, so why all the cursing?

The Lyla sleeping in the theater couldn't pull off this move. That's why her audition was so *safe*; she wasn't sure on her feet. This move requires balance, technical skill, and control. She's no longer so thin I worry she's starving, and seeing how she hasn't resisted my efforts, I know how thin she'd gotten wasn't by her own choice.

When it doesn't go her way once again, she curses under her breath and turns to her phone to stop the music, but her hand freezes when she sees me.

Her delicate throat works down a lump, and she brushes a rogue strand of hair out of her face. "You left it open."

I nod, a little thrill zipping through me that she was nervous about my reaction. She smiles a little, and I nearly return the gesture. She's so good for me. I don't say anything, but I don't move away either. Deep inside, I always knew if I opened this place to her, it meant me coming in too. I can't imagine having this woman dance in my home and not being here to watch, but I'm still unsure about it.

My grip on her costume is tight, and my amusement is not enough to take away my nerves entirely. I take a long breath before my foot crosses the threshold, and I'm inside once again. My concentration rests on her, not the memories or the humiliating spiderweb crack. My eyes hungrily trace my favorite features—all of them. But especially the small beauty mark beside her nose. The way she bites the inside of the cheek and the cluster of light freckles dancing across her shoulders.

I hand her the costume, my movements robotic before I step away and give her space, leaning over the piano with my arms crossed over my chest.

Beckoning her to take the last few steps to me, I hand her an ensemble I never imagined her wearing. The costume is beautiful and layered, but it looks like the others, and nothing you'd catch the star dancing in. She's just one of many on the stage, yet her face lights up when she looks at it. I push it toward her a little more forcefully and nod my head for her to try it on.

She pulls it off the plastic hanger, inspecting the inside.

"And you're going to watch?"

"Mm." The sound is one of affirmation and excitement. I fucking love her body.

I don't move. Of course I'm going to watch as she takes her clothes off. Nothing in the world would make me miss my favorite show. She rolls her eyes, but her cheeks are pink with the flattery. Little by little, Lyla is coming out of her shell. She's so far outside my normal preference and nothing like I told myself she would be when I was obsessed with her body and dancing but not the woman beneath.

Her smiles, giggles, and willingness to push me make me feel more alive than ever. For years, I've told myself I prefer obedience and things in their place, but I've never been more inspired than when surrounded by her brand of disorder.

She pushes the leotard straps down her shoulders, and I completely lose my train of thought. It doesn't matter how many times I see her body, it always feels like the first time. She reveals her body slowly, first her breasts with her rosy pink nipples, so beautiful and delicate, already peaked in stiff little points.

Her soft, flat belly next, then her pretty pussy puts itself on display, begging to be licked. The gift I bought for her after I finger fucked her on the barre pools around her feet. She kicks them out of the way and excitedly climbs into the costume.

She turns from me to the mirror, tilting her head as she watches herself. Her big brown eyes are sparkling with a million questions behind them. The red looks perfect against her pale blond hair. It makes me want to buy her a wardrobe of red dresses so I can rip them from her body.

"Do you like it?"

"I'll like it better when you nail the fouetté turns."

Her mouth opens in shocked offense like she can't believe what I just said. It shouldn't be a surprise. I expect a lot from her.

"Mikhail!" She makes a face like she's not taking me seriously and turns back to the mirror. "I can't believe you hurt your jaw just to say that to my face."

Making sure she reaches her full potential is the best use of my jaw. I don't say that. Instead, I make a sign for her to take it from the top, and I sit on the piano bench.

It takes her only a second of confusion, but then she walks to the center of the room to start. I'm rusty and not the same pianist I once was, but this composition poured out of my soul. It's not something I learned, but what I am. Even if I forget all the music in the world, I'd still know how to play this as long as I live.

Lyla tips her chin up, feet in first position and arms in fifth. She's ready. I start the section quickly, and the Fouetté turns need to follow the rhythm. She gets to three on time, but her fourth is delayed. She knows it, so she doesn't bother with the fifth.

She's back in first position. Determination sets into lines on her face as she nods at me, asking me to run through it once again.

That's my girl.

CHAPTER 21
LYLA
ACT 2

MY EGO BRUISES at the realization of how far my skills have slipped. I can't blame it on hunger or exhaustion when neither is true. I'm just unpracticed. What once was instinct is now labor. I'm weaker and slower, someone I don't recognize. This person doesn't deserve to dance for Mikhail. I remind myself this is not who I am. This starved and lonely version of me is only temporary. All the things I once did, I can do them again.

I just need to keep pushing.

I pick up the pace and try the Fouetté turns once again. I tell myself I deserve the grace of not being perfect while homeless and starving. I should forgive myself if no one else in this city will. That time has ended. I'm fed, and I'm ready to fight for what is mine.

My landing is graceful, but I'm half a count behind, and that's an eternity to a ballerina. I don't even spare Mikhail a glance. We don't need to tell each other what happens next. We both know. We are doing this until I get it right.

Having Mikhail in the room with me is the push I need. I blame this need for perfection on him, but I might be even worse.

This is mine.

My leg whips around, and I count my turns. One, two, three. *I'm on time.*

Four, five, and six.

Land.

I end the movement with my right foot perfectly behind my left. Mikhail stops playing and looks at me. He doesn't smile or shower me with praise, yet I breathe a little lighter. I did it.

Of course, I just accomplished what any ballerina worth their salt is capable of. If I want to earn my place, I need to keep pushing. We both need more than that. I'm back to the center of the room, and he begins the piece from the top.

The red tulle sticks to my damp legs. My confidence grows with each step, and I flash a look to Mikhail. The music ascends, and while this is my cue to step away and give room to his prima ballerina, I dance her part in this studio.

Electricity runs free through my body, the excitement uncurling from the pit of my stomach to every extremity. The music flows within me. I feel it when my heart beats fast with the rhythm. I don't miss a step, and I don't doubt myself.

My beautiful grand jeté lands me on the other side of the room. I step to the side and don't even glance at Mikhail. This part is not from his production. I know his prima ballerina can't deliver this.

My lips curl just a little at the corner before I start again with the Fouettés.

Just half an hour ago, I couldn't get the seven right, but now I embark on the thirty-two sequence that earned me a standing ovation every night when I performed *Swan Lake*. I'm transported in time. With each turn, a piece of Lyla reattaches, and I keep pushing. The only thing that could stop me now is the movement of his fingers on the keys.

He keeps playing, following my lead, and presses the

melody, urging my turns all the way to the end, and I finish strong for him with an arabesque.

He plucks the last note, and silence engulfs both of us. My breathing is the only thing I hear. Mikhail stays silent as he turns around on the piano bench to fully face me.

We watch each other from across the room. I'm breathless in the best way possible like a piece of clear blue sky puzzle just clicked into place. His eyes cut, narrowing as he looks at me, but I know what I just did. I don't know if I can repeat this every night like I used to, but I did it this once.

And it was fucking perfect.

He brings his hand to his jaw, the pad of his thumb grazing his bottom lip. The way he looks at me takes the air out of my lungs, undoing all that poise I just had. I'm waiting for his response—maybe his opinion of the moves I added to his routine or hopefully the praise I'm so hungry for.

"Crawl to me," his rough voice demands.

The temperature in the room changes as heat runs up and down my body. My eyes widen in surprise, lust, and desperation to please him. I thought I'd done that, but I guess there's one last hoop for me to crawl through.

"What?"

But he just stares, telling me he knows I heard. If there's a man alive worth pleasing, it's Mikhail. I sink to my knees, my beating heart pulsing in my ears. The room is silent except for the rustling of tulle as I crawl to him.

He leans back over the piano, staring at me with a hunger that makes me want to run to him.

"Slowly," he insists, and that permanent crease between his brows softens.

I obey him, slinking across the floor, slow and sultry. By the time I'm kneeling in front of him, my mouth is dry. I don't even notice the hard floor under me. He takes his hard cock out, and I have to sink my teeth into my bottom lip to hold back my moan of excitement.

He pumps his cock in his hands, forcing me to watch when I want so badly to actively participate. My eyes hungrily trace his working forearm as he strokes his cock.

His tip leaks precum. He gathers it on the pad of his thumb and paints my lips with it like it's expensive lipstick.

"Don't," he cautions me, but I quickly ignore him, my tongue darting out for a taste. My eyes slip closed as I moan, and much to my shock, a light slap lands on my cheek. "I said don't," he growls.

I stare deep into his eyes as I lick up the rest. I don't even care if I'm too needy. All I care about is pleasing him. He takes my jaw and chin between his fingers and then closes his hand around my neck.

I gasp, not expecting the move so quickly after that little smack.

"My ballerina, my pretty doll. Under all that tulle, you're just a wet, willing whore."

I wish I could argue, but my god, he's right.

He nudges me up. His hand is warm and familiar, and my pulse quickens as I await his next move. He pushes me over the piano, drawing a loud and abrupt sound from the keys. I place one foot on the stool, trying to hold myself up. His other hand goes for my knee, stopping the attempt and smacking my ass down loudly. He follows up gently, smoothing over my thigh. I stop breathing altogether.

I flashback to the first time he touched me over the barre. Just like that, I'm drenched for him again, excited and scared of what he's capable of doing to me.

So much like that time, he reaches the edge of my leotard, gently teasing the edge of my pussy. My breath comes shallow as he pushes the fabric to the side and runs his fingers up and down, spreading that wetness from my entrance to my clit.

"Please, Mikhail, please," I whine before he finally gives in and thrusts two fingers inside my pussy.

He pumps into me, igniting my insides. "Talk dirty to me."

"What?"

"All I want to do is fill your ears with filth, but you don't want me to hurt myself, right?"

He stares deep into my eyes, waiting for me to answer. "Right," I agree.

"So do it for me."

"Fuck, I want you." I lick my lips, thinking about what he wants from me. I'm not experienced, but I know what I want. I know what turns me on to some extent. "Fuck me, Mikhail."

He brings his thumb over my clit. "More."

My head falls back. This impossible man always wants too much.

"I need to feel your cock splitting me open. Please." I'm whining so desperately that tears are next.

He shakes his head.

"Mikhail." I try to bat my eyes, but he just smirks at me. Suddenly, I realize what he wants. "I'm your dirty little ballerina whore, and all I want is to dance for you and give you my pussy. Will you please make me your whore, Mikhail?"

Something feral takes over him, and the fingers pumping inside me quickly move to my mouth. He shoves them deep into my throat, making me gag, but instead of pulling back, I lap my taste off him. I use the task of sucking his fingers to distract myself from my desperation as he lines the head of his cock up with my entrance.

He slides home in one move. I'm so turned on I don't need a lot more stimulation than his cock stretching me open. He's impossibly big like this, and I have to try to widen my lips to take him all.

With each thrust, the piano keys sing. His balls slap against my wet thighs, making a mess of me and his gorgeous instrument. I moan even louder than the discordant notes.

He takes my pussy as seriously as he did his composition

as he played. Bringing my legs up, I give him deeper access. My whimpers mix with his grunts. Dampness coats my skin and sticks the two of us together. I shout his name until my voice goes hoarse as his hips slap relentlessly against my ass. I'm his.

I'm so perfectly his, so entirely his.

He must see it on my face because he's suddenly much closer to the edge. I'm nothing if not a willing whore for him, so as he gets closer, I get closer too. When he comes, I come with him, and we're left tangled together in a sweaty pile on top of his piano.

When he steps away, his cum drips down my legs, staining all the pretty red tulle.

CHAPTER 22
LYLA
ACT 2

THE LIGHTS BURN MY BACK, and the curtain hangs closed in front of us. Discordant strands of music start to play, notes of sorrow plucked from Mikhail's own compositions. Chills break out across my body, the music so intimate now that I know what it means. The responsibility to convey all that emotion to the audience overwhelms me, and I'm hardly the star tonight.

The entire cast stands in place for the start of the show, each of us dressed in gauzy white that will spin around us as we move, the first of three costumes that will shift darker as the show moves on—the red tule is my final costume.

I stand at the back, warming my legs by performing a series of dégagés. My body no longer screams its complaints when I try basic moves. The rest and practice I received at Mikhail's were enough to make me an athlete again. That routine I danced last night has me feeling close to a comeback.

The music changes, and I school my face in the position of soft sadness he demanded of this dance. Curtains rise, and the hot lights are momentarily twice as bright and blinding before my eyes adjust, and they slightly soften. Moving through the choreography, I find my steps on time, my movements soft.

It's hard to believe the Lyla dancing today is the same person who struggled to keep up with the other dancers just a few weeks ago. I should be proud of myself at this moment when my pirouette finishes in perfect timing with everyone else, yet I'm aching with a deep sense of hollowness.

Part of it is an echo of Mikhail's grief, written into each note of this song, but there's more, a sense that I'll never be good enough again. It doesn't matter how good I am now. I'll never deserve to dance for a man like him.

I exit stage left when the performance is done. It's time for the prima ballerina's solo and for me to change costumes. I watch her dance a moment too long, sinking in the powerlessness of my situation. Too much was taken from me when Carter spread his lies. I remember the moment I realized what was happening and watched as my dreams slipped through my fingers.

That weight hangs on me as I change costumes into the one I wore while I crawled to him. It only takes me a moment. I'm well practiced, but the memories make my cheeks hot.

I'm back in time to watch the end of her solo. The other ballerinas are too, their eyes hungrily latched on Judith. I won't pretend to know their thoughts, but their expressions don't seem kind.

I remember that burn on the back of your neck when too many people are watching with negative intentions. I decide then and there not to be one of the ones wishing on her downfall, no matter how much I wish I were in her place.

Her moves are beautiful and strong, yet perhaps a little stiff if I'm being perfectly honest. But I immediately regret the thought. It's not fair to judge her like that. There's a reason I'm backstage right now, and she's in the spotlight.

Mikhail choreographed an otherworldly dance, and while it's dark and haunting, something is so distinctly Christmas and winter about the whites, reds, and silvers of this production. I'm touched by the beauty he's managed to weave, but my heart aches because if things were the way they should have been, I would be center stage right now.

She finishes, holding an arabesque with sheer swathes of fabric hanging around her, giving her the impression of a snowflake when the lights shine through the shimmering panels. The lights lower to black, and the scene changes.

The ballet continues in a similar fashion. I dance as best I can, doing surprisingly well, changing costumes, watching in envy and sadness as someone else performs the art Mikhail crafted.

Do I love him?

I shouldn't be thinking about this now, but now that the question has snaked its way into my mind and heart, I can't shake it off. How I feel isn't fair as I watch Judith perform like she stole something from me.

She didn't.

If anyone stole from me, that was Carter. It's not fair of me to feel like she's dancing my solo and performing art from the soul of the man I love, but I do. Would I prefer if he had fucked her? If this was just his ex. Yes, I decide. Sex feels trivial compared to this, but this is his soul, and another woman's body is expressing it.

I want to be sick.

The time passes in strange lurches as I give my all to the choreography he's asked me to perform, and then the same effort to watching his prima ballerina like it's her fault I wasn't strong enough for the part.

"Lyla, are you okay?" Maeve asks as I'm changing into my final costume, the red number I tried for Mikhail.

"Of course, why? Do I look bad?" I turn around and look over my shoulder, checking the tulle for any trace of his cum.

"Oh no, stop. You're great. You just seem… off, I guess."

"I'm fine," I promise her with a fake smile as I move into position for the final dance of the show.

Our cue arrives, and we rush on the stage, creating a flurry of black-and-red-like feathers. I forget my jealousy and concerns and put everything into doing Mikhail's production justice. It doesn't matter what's happened between the two of us or how close it feels we've gotten. I need to do this right to keep from disappointing him.

Sometimes I wonder if I can die from the weight of his displeasure alone.

When the song ends, the audience erupts in applause. An electric wave pulses as the crowd stands. All my thoughts evaporate, and suddenly, I'm in this moment. My heart hammers inside my chest, and the lights burn my face. A small drop of sweat drips between my breasts, and I close my eyes, taking it all in.

A tear rolls down my cheek for all the emotions colliding inside me. I'm sad for what I've lost and now understand that coming back doesn't magically fix things. Being on this stage isn't the same as leading the production.

But I'm happy too. I'm glad that I'm here and standing. I'm proud of my body even though it's not doing what it used to do. It's doing *something*.

The show ends, and the lights dim, leaving space for us to head backstage. I look for my bag in the sea of excited ballerinas and find someone moved it off the bench in front of my cubby and onto the ground. I'm about to grab it when I hear that low grit that makes my panties melt every time.

"Lyla," he says, and I turn to find him staring at me. Everyone falls silent, except for one titter of expectation that I'm about to get in trouble.

I stare at him, fifteen sets of eyes flicking between us both, waiting to see what happens. I'm so on edge I may collapse, but I can't stop staring. His gaze is all-consuming, icy-blue eyes that cut and soothe at once. Instead of saying any more, ordering them out so he can finger fuck me, or whatever megalomaniacs do, he strides toward me.

I count the ten steps he takes before he reaches me. Not saying a word, he pulls my chin up with the tips of his fingers and forces me to look him in the eyes.

"I am so proud of you."

And then his lips are on mine, in front of everyone.

His mouth is hard and warm, his beard recently shaved but rough against my skin. He doesn't have the ability to move his jaw easily, so there's never more than a simple pass of his tongue, but the depth and intensity of how his lips press against mine is unmatched by any other kiss in existence. I'm sure of it.

Shocked gasps echo around us, but they don't say a word. You'd have to be really stupid to actually talk shit about Mikhail in hearing range. I'm lost in him; my hands smooth the fabric of his shirt, and I feel his hot skin underneath.

He pulls back, offering me the slightest bend of his lips. Is it a smile? My insides warm to the point of bursting when he takes my hand and leads me out without any attention paid to anyone else. We're on the dark set of stairs that leads between the stage, the dressing room, and the street exit, when I turn and kiss him again. I move away from his lips to his cheek, then his jaw, and one on his neck.

"Aw, isn't this sweet," an achingly familiar, aristocratic voice speaks from the partial darkness at the bottom of the stairs.

What the hell is he doing here?

Carter watches us, his face showing the depths of his anger for the first time. His presence is an intense violation. I'm sick to my stomach, knowing what he wanted from me.

My fingers wind around Mikhail's arm, desperate for him to keep me safe. This time, Carter won't touch me.

"Do not speak to her," Mikhail spits in a low, dangerous

tone that raises the hair on the back of my neck, but he doesn't seem surprised to see Carter like I am.

"What is he doing here, Mikhail?"

He hides his pain a little too well. I don't like that he's so practiced at ignoring his own suffering, and right now I'm sure he's using that practice to hide something from me as well.

"I'll speak to my errant stepdaughter however I please, Mikhail, especially when she's worsening her own terrible reputation." He turns his gaze back to me. "When did you get so lazy that you don't even check which productions are running? I've been here for weeks."

I turn and stare at Mikhail, uncharacteristic anger aimed at him. Everything suddenly clicks into place, and his need to take me home, and keep me from the theater seems far less noble.

The mention of my reputation triggers me, as well as finding out I've been lied to and manipulated, but only one of them is really a villain. Carter did this. He ruined me and my career. This fucking pervert wanted me when I was a child. Mikhail might be toxic, but at he has my best interest at heart.

"I'm sorry," he presses his lips to my ear and I already know I won't be holding a grudge.

"I'm not your stepdaughter." Righteous indignation burns through my system as I stare at Carter's graying hair, brown eyes, and the shoulders I cried on as a girl. "You lost the right to call me that when you tried to fuck me."

Carter's mouth drops open like he's truly shocked and offended. His head shakes in that dismissive way that has always fucked with my sense of reality. Like it's obvious I'm the one lying.

"If that's the case, then you don't mind if I start playing dirty?" He tips his head to the side, revealing far more of his insidious nature than I'm used to seeing in public. This is exactly why I won't be holding that grudge, I know what true evil looks like.

"Start?" Mikhail asks. "Carter, you've been dirty, and don't think *I* won't play back."

Carter shoots Mikhail a ferocious look. I instinctively tremble, knowing what kind of trouble I would be in as a kid if he looked at me that way.

"I have far more connections in this city than you do, this theater even. I would think twice about challenging me. Pity over your accident will only extend so far," Carter says.

Carter turns on his heel, and I see red, briefly considering actually attacking him. If he thinks he's had the last word, he's wrong.

Carter's success comes from his connections, and I understand that now. His productions are uninspired and repetitive. He's small, petty, boring, and there isn't a single opinion he holds that matters.

"Carter," I say. He turns halfway back. "Do remember, you can make up lies about me, but I know some very frightening truths about you. You have so very much more to lose than I do."

"You're a whore, Lyla. I'm not afraid of you."

Mikhail balls his hand into a fist, but I grab his arm and beg him with my eyes to do nothing as Carter leaves, feeling like he's won.

He hasn't fucking won.

CHAPTER 23
MIKHAIL
ACT 2

WE CLIMB INTO THE CAR, and for once, I'm shaking with rage instead of fear. I can't remember the last time I was in a car and didn't hold my breath as we pulled away, yet somehow, this isn't better.

I should have said more. I should have done more. Carter doesn't deserve to breathe after everything. But what was I going to do? It's not like I could beat him to death in the theater like I would have liked. I'd wind up in jail and banned from hosting any show there. I've never been particularly violent. I boxed and wrestled in school, but I didn't need blood.

Lyla is changing everything about me, taking me from a refined upper-crust gentleman and turning me into an animal who will fuck and fight in the dirt for what's mine. My knuckles scream from how tightly I'm clenching my fists, as does my jaw. The bones and muscles are destroyed, yet I still can't eliminate my innate reaction to stress, which is clenching those muscles.

"Fucking, goddammit," I seethe.

The words are like shards of glass splitting my jaw. Tonight, I'm too angry to hold it all in. Sometimes a man just needs to say what he feels, and maybe I'm tired of keeping myself protected, watching my words, and staying silent. I never had to do any of that before the accident. Yes, I spent my life rich and spoiled and handsome enough to get whatever else I wanted that money couldn't buy, but I've had to learn how to be an entirely different man since then.

Why the fuck is Carter Livingston enough to shake any shreds of my confidence? He shouldn't be, but he is. My mind plays different scenarios, pushing me to do something before he has time to spill more lies.

A soft hand reaches out and touches my jaw, and my eyes fall closed.

"Stop it. You're hurting yourself."

My body is on the edge. Even her touch hurts, but I need it too. Her hands trace my jawline, and her perfume floats in the air. She coaxes me to relax, and much to my surprise, my body responds, loosening the worst of the tension.

"What can I do?" she asks.

Images of having Carter dead come to mind, but that's not something Lyla can deliver. I wonder if this is how she feels, too. I wonder if she hates him as much as I do or if a part of her still loves him and is bleeding for his lies.

"Tell me he's nothing," I challenge.

"You know he's nothing. I hate him. I l—"

I can't pretend I'm not alarmed by whatever she was about to say, but that's not what I want to hear. That's not what's tearing me up right now. Lyla turns to me, her eyes set on mine, her hand over my cheek.

"He isn't half the artist you are. He doesn't have your vision. Carter Livingston is nothing." Her fingers move down my neck to my chest. Her words finally release me from this insecurity tearing me apart. "You're so angry."

I just nod.

"I've never had someone so angry on my behalf before,"

she informs me, clearly not knowing this is far from the first time I've been like this as a direct result of her.

Doesn't she know I'd be the living dead if it weren't for her? Doesn't she understand I'm hollowed and beyond repair. All of my feelings are because of her.

Her fingers keep moving down to the crotch of my pants, where she finds I'm already hard. Even in anger, I can't stop myself from wanting Lyla. Her pretty face furrows in confusion—she just doesn't understand how badly I want her. She brings me to the edge and then straight over it. Wanting this woman is the most dangerous thing I've ever done because not having her would truly kill me. She shreds everything I thought I knew about myself.

"Being near you makes me fucking crazy." That's the best way to make sense of it. It's a simple equation: the closer I am to Lyla, the more I am a need-driven animal, and the less I am a civilized man raised in his society. She has me ready to fuck or fight at a moment's notice.

She blinks slowly, her mouth parting like this is the first time she's ever considered such a thing, and I wonder how she could be so clueless. Everything I am is centered around her; the atoms of my being have realigned to make space for her. From the first time I saw Lyla, I knew we were meant to be together.

"You make me crazy too. I always want you when I shouldn't. I live for your attention, Mikhail."

Fuck, my cock pulses as she speaks. I don't give a fuck how toxic it is. I want every breath she takes to be for me, with thoughts of me. I want to see her as crazy as she makes me. I don't put her mind at ease and let her know my attention is always on her.

It doesn't matter what room we are in and how many people are talking; my eyes will follow Lyla wherever she goes. I keep that information to myself because I want to keep her hungry. You work hard for the things you want most, and her working for my attention is beyond fucking delicious. It's everything.

Her delicate fingers play with my zipper, and I only watch, not telling her what to do today. She looks down and then back up at me. He innocent look asks permission, but I keep my face devoid of expression.

Lyla bites her fat lower lip, then undoes my pants and pulls my cock into her hands. I'm expecting her to suck me off or stroke me, but she shocks me when she pulls down her sweats. The divider between us and the driver sits closed, so our audience won't know anything is up unless we get too loud. Frankly, I want to show off how good it is to fuck her. Animals aren't private, are they? And that's exactly what she makes me.

She's all warm and soft skin, where I can feel her through my open pants. Reaching behind herself, she grabs my cock and lines me up with her entrance, wasting absolutely no time in lowering onto me and fucking me to the hilt. She's sitting in my lap, locked in place on my cock, and it couldn't be more satisfying after that confrontation.

"Shit, you're so good for me," I grit, grabbing twin fistfuls of her ass cheeks as she starts to bounce up and down on me. Blond hair spills over her back, and I wrap it around my hand several times as she moves.

She's so tight, so hot, and I'm so raw in my anger I could come right away, but I hold it in. If my pretty little slut wants to fuck, I need to let her. She starts to moan as she moves, a bit too loud if she doesn't want the driver to hear. My hand clamps over her mouth, stifling the worst of the noise. I want to be patient and let her keep fucking me at her own pace, but I shift up, thrusting into her, and the sound she makes vibrates against my palm. Oh, my pretty ballerina likes that.

She's still bouncing against me, but after every second or third bounce, I thrust back, hitting her G-spot and stretching her a little too deeply. I reach around, cupping her perfect little tits in my hands, and I can't help but notice they're fuller now that she's healthier. Taking her nipple between two of my fingers, I work her into a frenzy, drawing her closer to an orgasm with the sensitive nipples that helped me get so far in fucking her in her sleep.

"Mikhail, tell me you're with me. You're not thinking of anything but this."

My perfect ballerina whore is all I ever think about. I dream about her pussy and feel the phantom grip of her walls around me when she's not near. She has me completely. How is she the only one who can't see it?

"Just you," I say, and her cunt clenches. This time, I don't bother to muffle her shout, letting her come long and loud for our driver and anyone on the street to hear.

I follow her by a half beat, filling her tight little pussy up with my cum in thick pleasurable spurts. We sit together unmoving for a minute. My cock softens, filling her with cum, and then hardens again.

She giggles and starts to fuck me more, but we're nearly back to the apartment. I stop her hips and hold up my finger, letting her know I'll be more than happy to give her more when I take her inside. I pull her off my cock and slide her little panties back into place, liking how cum-soaked they're going to be.

We ride the elevator to the penthouse. Lyla rests her head on my shoulder, letting out a satisfied sigh. I'm glad my cock was enough for her to forget what happened back in the theater, but I can't say I've forgotten my concerns.

The season is off to a strong start, but that only means there's more to lose. I never considered Carter dangerous, but something was very threatening about how he addressed Lyla, and I don't like it. I'll have to keep a close eye on him and everyone in the theater.

CHAPTER 24
LYLA
FINALE

REHEARSAL BEGINS, and I can't help but notice the watching eyes or the murmur of voices. What bothered me when I first arrived at this theater doesn't anymore. What they say about me now is true. I am with Mikhail. He drives me and brings me back home. We fuck in his car, bed, and kitchen. My skills aren't disintegrating under their watchful eyes because what comes out of their mouths is true, and that's the difference.

Eduard divides the production into sections, each group in different rooms and timetables. In the morning, I still start early and warm up at the barre, making sure to stretch. In the afternoon, I bounce between two groups, and each time, I surprise myself and others with excellence.

Maeve is usually around, the only one who isn't scared to approach me. We eat together and run routines side by side. She always smiles and thanks me when I point out things she can do to better her craft. It's a far cry from what it used to be for me.

Eventually, Eduard comes to stand nearby, specifically paying attention to me. He doesn't tut or click his tongue, and

I'm nearly ten feet tall as I land the final move of my routine for the performance later tonight.

"Very good, Lyla. You nailed your performance last night too." Eduard doesn't give compliments he doesn't mean, and no one snickers or otherwise signifies they disagree. I hold my head high, and for once, I am sure I can be proud of myself.

Rehearsal comes to a close, and we have a two-hour break before we have to be back for costumes and makeup. I plan to get something to eat and hopefully track down Mikhail. He's created this desperation in me I can hardly understand. His attention and his affection—I need them both more than I need air. *I hope he's pleased with me tonight.*

"Lyla." Someone calls my name, and I turn to find the prima ballerina, Judith.

"Hey, Judith," I say carefully. She's smiling, but she's never been anything else other than snickering every time we crossed paths.

"You really are doing amazing."

My shoulders relax, and I release my anxiety for a minute. Everyone notices how hard I've been working. My improvement is the most obvious thing about this production. Sure, we won't be best friends, but maybe she appreciates my dedication.

"Thanks," I breathe, still unsure where this is going.

"How did you improve so fast? You were really rough when we started."

Her eyes flash with a mean glint that takes me back to our first week together. My eyebrows come together as I frown. It's not exactly something you can explain.

"Just needed to get back to the old me, I guess."

I step back, desperate to get away from her and end this conversation. "I have to go now. I promised…"

"I'm going this way, too." She falls into line with my steps, clearly not taking the hint. "You *were* the best. You know it really gets old hearing your name all the time."

My heart rate increases. What the hell does she want? She's the star now. Does she just need to rub it in?

"It has been a couple of hard years." There's no use denying it when she and the others saw all my things in my car at the beginning of the month. I don't care what her problem is. The results are all that matter. Look how I've managed to turn things around.

Lies can ruin someone's career, destroy their mental health, and anyone can be next. It happened to me and could happen to them too—lots of men lie. She's surprised how good I've gotten? Does she think I have a secret recipe to share? I had to crawl my way back from hell. It might look sudden, but it cost a hell of a lot more than she can imagine.

Judith nods, and for a second, I think she understands what I mean.

"It was pretty great to see you humbled."

My mouth falls open, and I turn to her, stopped in my tracks. Her lips crack a small smile like we're sharing a joke, but I'm not laughing.

"What the fuck do you want?" I demand, but before she answers, I pick up the pace, ready to leave her behind.

"What I want is for you to go away. I don't want to have to compete with some slut who would fuck her own stepfather."

Of course. I turn around, and she's following me so closely I almost bump into her. "How am I competition to you? You're the prima ballerina, you lunatic!"

"Isn't this why you're fucking Mikhail Ivanov now?" She pushes me. "You are known for fucking your way to the top. I won't let you ruin this for me."

"Don't talk about what you don't know, Judith." My voice is low, but I hope she hears the threat behind my words.

I turn around to follow the path to Mikhail's office, but Judith blocks me. "How is that fair? I worked hard too!"

"You got the lead role. What more do you want?"

"There are more shows, Lyla. The lead is mine."

"Fine!"

There's no alternative but to turn and go the other way. At this point, I don't care if I have to go around the block and call Mikhail from outside. All I want is to avoid her. I wouldn't dare tell her I was a virgin before him. She can think I'm the whore of Babylon for all I care. She's not worth my breath. If anything, I learned people can say whatever they want. It only matters if you let it.

And I don't.

"Fuck you!" I shout at the top of my lungs, ready to sprint away from her if that's what I have to do.

An alleyway only theater workers use to load and unload materials stands to my right. I slap the door in anger and go outside. Cold air sweeps my hair and stings my cheeks. I'm annoyed I'm out in the cold without a jacket, angry that people like Judith still think they can talk to me however they please.

My head hangs, and I take a breath, deciding whether I call Mikhail from here or go inside and throttle Judith. I reach for the door, but before my hand closes on the knob, someone calls my name.

"Lyla, baby." His voice chills my blood, and I look up to find Carter watching me with an expression of fake concern. "What are you doing out here? You don't have a coat."

I thought his production had ended. All their stuff is gone, so he has no business being here yet again. He comes closer, and I step back, a reaction that doesn't go unnoticed. His lips close in a flat line, but he shakes it away, schooling his expression.

"This rebellion phase. It's gone too far now."

My mouth opens, and I snap it closed. I want to argue and

ask what the fuck he's talking about, but I should know better than to argue with crazy. I go for the door again, but he's faster. Arms snap around me, holding me much too tight.

"Lyla." He sighs. "It's time to come home, baby."

"Let me go. What's wrong with you?" I scream.

I struggle against him, but he doesn't let me go, and my desperation reaches a new high. His arms bring me even closer, and I feel his erection digging into my belly, and bile rises up my throat.

"No, no, Carter, let me go!" I'm begging, desperate, and with the image of my mother in my mind's eye, I start crying. A car rolls slowly forward, but I only pay the slightest attention to it as I fight to add space between his body and mine.

My struggle increases, but I'm no match for him. He lifts me easily, and even as I scream, I know the sound won't penetrate the dense walls of the theater. He starts walking toward the car I noticed but hadn't paid much attention to.

Oh fuck, he's taking me.

"Mikhail!" I know he can't hear me, but tell that to my frantic heart.

He opens the door and shoves us both inside while someone else hits the gas. By the time the door shuts, we're moving much too fast for me to escape. Carter's eyes are wild when our gazes meet.

"Don't ever say his name again."

I shake, my heart hammers, and I look around as if I could find a way to escape this moving vehicle. My nails dig into the leather seat when reality hits me.

There's no escape.

Carter looks at me with brown eyes full of excitement. He doesn't even try to hide that he's looking at my body with lust.

"I've waited long enough. It's time I finally get what I want from you, Lyla."

The car speeds up, and thick dread pools in my stomach.

CHAPTER 25
MIKHAIL
FINALE

THE SHOW STARTS IN AN HOUR, so I head backstage to ensure my ballerinas are in place and prepared or about to be. I'm desperate to see one in particular, but when I step inside, I find a ruckus.

Dancers are panicking, talking to one another, calling, and typing on their phones. When they see me, they all freeze at once, with looks of true fear. I'm accustomed to them looking at me a certain way, but something about this makes all my alarms ring.

"What's happening?"

They all flinch when I ask. This is the most I've ever said in front of them. None of the ballerinas are ready for the sound of my voice. I scan their faces, wondering which one is brave enough to tell me.

"Judith is gone," one in the back says, her face pink.

For a second, I almost ask who the fuck Judith is, but then I remember she's my prima ballerina. I nod, but right then, another pipes up.

"How on earth is the show supposed to go on without her? She doesn't have an understudy."

While not having my primary performer might be

concerning for someone worried about their ballet, I couldn't give less of a fuck, and it's all down to the fact Lyla is not in this room.

"Where is Lyla?"

My girl is never late. She loves her job, and she knows I expect her to deliver the best. One hour until curtain? She should be in this room warming up.

"She's not here," the one ballerina who has been kind to Lyla finally says.

She looks concerned, holding her phone tight. I walk across the room, letting the girls return to their panic. There's only one I want anything from.

"Maeve, right?" She nods, shaking with nerves. "Do you know where Lyla is?"

"I've been calling her. It rang a couple of times, but now I'm getting nothing like she turned off her phone."

I swallow the fear that statement leaves me with. "When did you last see her?"

"A little over an hour ago. She said she was leaving to get some lunch and find you…" Her brows push together as she realizes what she's saying. "I guess she didn't find you, then."

No, she did not. I don't say it out loud. I'm too consumed by the worry settling in my chest to force myself to speak through the pain.

Where the hell is Lyla?

"Judith was talking to Lyla," one of the girls says.

I turn to their group, and another girl shakes her head.

"They never talk, so that makes no sense."

"I'm telling you. It's not like I don't know what Judith and Lyla look like."

They are easily the most known in the bunch. Judith is tall and easy to spot; Lyla is short, but her pale blond hair sticks out in a crowd. Suddenly, Judith's disappearance is my concern. After everything I put into my work, having no show today is the least of my concerns. It's all about Lyla.

Eduard arrives, and all the dancers flock around him to tell him what's happening. I leave him to deal with them and head up to the office, where I know there's a security system. It's rudimentary and doesn't have sound, but it's my lifeline now.

I flick through the cameras, finding Lyla finally in the dressing room a couple of hours earlier. I follow her until I can't see her anymore, then I switch to the next camera for a better angle, pausing the moment Judith approaches Lyla. They talk, and it looks like a normal conversation other than Lyla's body language saying she's uncomfortable.

My hand closes in a fist as their conversation clearly turns into an argument. Judith gives Lyla a mean smile, and Lyla tries to get away from her. Ultimately, Lyla leaves alone through the side door.

Moving through the cameras until I find the one showing the back door, I wait for the moment Lyla returns, but it never comes. Snow still falls outside, and she's missing her jacket. An hour later, she's still not back, and then we're back at the present.

My phone pings, and I check to find a message from Eduard. Judith is back, but Lyla is not. *Where the fuck is Lyla?*

I fly down the stairs, back to the dressing room, and find the ballerinas fawning over the snake who chased Lyla outside.

"Come. Now."

If my control snaps any further, I may just kill her. Each of the girls steps back except Judith. They all know exactly who I'm speaking to. I wonder if any of them were involved.

She follows me out into the hall, and I lead her just far enough away that no one should hear our conversation. Turning on her, I cage her against the wall and aim to intimidate her. I'd never hit a woman—other than a naughty smack that Lyla enjoys—but I will literally fucking murder her in cold blood if she hurt Lyla.

"You are fired from this production." I speak very slowly and quietly, which helps. "If you want a chance to work anywhere in this city again, you will tell me exactly where *my* prima ballerina is. If you don't, I'll make sure you sink far lower than she ever did."

A fine tremor shakes her whole body, and she swallows a few times. Crocodile tears fall down her cheeks, and I despise her even more for trying to look innocent.

"It was Carter Livingston. I don't know where he took her. Hell, I didn't even know he was going to take her. He offered me money to get her outside, and I did, but I didn't know he was going to throw her in the car like that. I thought she wanted to go with him."

It takes everything inside me not to hurt her. Not only did she work with Carter but she assumed Lyla *wanted* him?

"Call him, find out where they are."

"I can't," she cries. "He's never given me his number or anything. I don't work for him. He just wanted me to get her outside."

"You're done."

I turn and leave her there. *Where the hell would Carter take her?*

I pick apart all the things Lyla told me about her creepy stepfather, trying to figure out where the hell they went. I could involve the police, but I don't want their involvement. The waters are already muddied by the rumors he's spread, and we don't need an audience to see how this all ends.

No, this is personal. He took what belongs to me too many fucking times now. I'd like to choke him with my own hand, and the police's presence might interrupt things.

He's a pervert. He told her he married her mother just for a chance to be with her, and he met her when she was twelve. How did that happen, exactly? She never really said. I pull up my phone and search the local theater records. Her first show in the area would have been when she was about ten. Did he see her there first and pursue her mother as a result?

So many disturbing things must have happened for what he said to be true.

His endgame has always been Lyla—owning Lyla, grooming Lyla. In the grand scheme of things, I want all of those things too, but I'm not a fucking pedophile. I want her because she's magnificent, and I enjoy seeing her thrive. She's the most talented ballerina in the world, and I need to make her shine.

I might not be anyone's Prince Charming, but I'm not like that sick fuck. He probably built a lot of fantasies about her over the years after living in the same house. I'm repulsed to think what things he could have done to get his jollies that she wouldn't have known about.

Each minute that passes without Lyla, the insidious feeling in my chest settles further. There's no way this ends without me killing him. The more I think about Carter and the life he led with Lyla's mom, the more I'm certain I should start looking at their shared home. Maybe he wants to live out some old fantasies. Perhaps he'll die for his fucking audacity.

CHAPTER 26
LYLA
FINALE

I SIT on the bed in my childhood room, but I don't feel safe like I used to in the good old days. I'm sick to my stomach. Everywhere I look, I find things I left behind when Carter threw me out. The precious memories I shared with my family before he entered the picture and ruined everything.

My mind can't help but trip over all the times he came into this room. All the nights he laid in the bed with me, saying he loved to put me to sleep. Tears stream down my face when I think how sick he was that whole time and what those seemingly innocent nights meant to him. How often did he take advantage of how naive and needy I was when he entered our lives?

It's not fair that he ruined my room for me, too. I can't look at its pale lavender walls without thinking about him. All the dance awards and trophies for other various activities and competitions don't take away from his constant influence. Some of my favorite dolls sit on high shelves, dusty, out of the way, and untouched for a long, long time. My heart breaks for the girl who used to live in this room and died when her mother did.

Carter hasn't only stained my memories and stolen my

childhood home, he made sure I never had time to sit and mourn my own mother like I should. She deserved that, and I did too.

Carter uses the same half knock he did when I was a kid, and it opens a second later. Carter smiles brightly as he walks inside. After all this time with Mikhail, I find his wide smile especially alarming. I'm afraid of him, truly afraid, for the first time in my life. When he hit on me, I was disgusted, ashamed, and hurt, but I never thought he might harm me or abduct me.

There's a sickness in that smile. The way he looks at me breaks my skin out in chills. It's cruel that he brought me here. This all feels too familiar on some level, and I'm scared to let my guard down. I keep thinking Carter has reached his limit of cruelty and depravity, but he keeps proving I underestimated him.

My body reacts to him before my brain. I make a frantic noise and kick, trying to put as much space between us as possible.

"Calm down, baby."

The pet name makes me want to die just to get away from him. He wasn't just a man who wanted to fuck me. He raised me, nurtured me—groomed me, for his own sick ends. *He always wanted me.*

The truth is, he did see my first, auditioning for his company.

"We'll take things slow." He promises me, talking low like he's too scared to frighten me, but he's savoring this.

Adrenaline spikes in my system, and my heart races. He comes to sit on the edge of the bed with a smile on his face.

"Let's start simple. How about a kiss?"

I don't answer and just stare at him with my mouth agape. He didn't say much to me on the ride over here, and I was too afraid to fight, knowing he's willing to at the very least spank me. Knowing what he must have gotten out of punishing me as a child makes my skin crawl.

"I said kiss me." His gaze hardens, and rage that I somehow never saw simmers just below the surface.

I don't know for sure what he will do when I reject him again, but I can't underestimate Carter. He'll beat the shit out of me, or he'll force me. I know it in my bones. Tears gather on my lashes, and I wish for just *one more* goddamn Christmas miracle.

The girl who slept in this bed believed in miracles, and I want to latch onto that version of me with all my might. I wish for Mikhail to save me, to come in and take me from this nightmare, but even as I try to have faith, I know this won't happen. We have a show tonight, and he probably doesn't even know I'm missing.

Carter's hand slides over, resting on my knee. If I could, I would turn my body inside out just to avoid his touch. His skin feels wrong and damp against mine. I try to shimmy away, but he only massages the muscle, forcing his touch on me.

Mikhail never asked for my permission, but I realize he had it all along. My body craves Mikhail, and my pleasure always meets his actions. When he looks at me, I feel seen. Maybe it's fucked up, but it's our fucked up way, and I'm addicted to us.

Carter's touch is a violation to me and my mother's memory. My skin crawls, and the longer he touches me, the more I know I can't endure that kiss.

"You're going to have to relax. This is very exciting for me. You might think fighting is a good idea, but I'll only like it more." Despite myself, my gaze flicks to his pants, and sure enough, he's hard.

He leans forward, dead set on closing the distance between us. I push him off, turning my body and trying like hell to get off the bed and away from him. It doesn't really work out in my favor. I'm half dangling off the bed as he wrestles with my lower half, his face presses into my ass, and I shriek at the top of my lungs in pure disgust.

"Get the fuck off me!" I shout.

I grab at the floor, trying to pull myself away. Random things wind up in my hands as I struggle, but the items from under my bed won't give me the purchase to escape.

Suddenly, I grip a set of silk ribbons, and I nearly toss them away before I realize what they are. *My first set of pointe shoes from when I was a little girl.* They're much smaller than what I wear now, but the slippers are just as hard with a solid toe made of densely packed paper and glue meant to lift and display the dancer—it's hard as fuck.

I grab the heel rather than the laces and swing backward, colliding the hard box in the toe with Carter's head. The blunt feeling of the strike travels up my arm and makes me squeamish, but it's better than him touching me. He curses at the first collision, dazed, but I waste no time. I hit him again and again, the combination of flesh and bone beneath my pointe a sensation I won't soon forget.

Finally, on the fourth strike, he's unconscious. He groans in his Lyla-induced sleep, and I know it won't last very long. I hit the pervert once more for luck before running out of the room and through the house. This is not how I wanted my last time in my childhood home to go.

I race past pictures of Mom and me that I wish I could grab, leaving behind things that meant a lot to us. I think about the ruby Christmas necklace. I don't have time for any of that when Carter is bound to wake up soon.

The front door stands twenty feet away when I hear him roar. He's been rejected and offended too many times, and he's coming for blood. I can feel it. Heavy footsteps echo down the hall at his approach, and I run to the front door, whimpering in true terror at what he will do.

My fingers grip the knob in relief, but it doesn't turn. *It's fucking locked.* The little knob does nothing but spin as I try to open it. His heavy footsteps echo down the stairs, and I look over my shoulder to catch him round the bottom. We make eye contact, and the moment my heart constricts painfully, he smiles wickedly.

"You little bitch, I'm going to fuck your ass raw for that."

I don't think twice. I reach for the table beside the door and throw Mom's favorite vase through the glass, shattering it. He just told me what he's going to do if he catches me, and I don't want to stick around to find out if he's lying. It's plenty tall and just wide enough for me to slip through with my clothes snagging and only a couple of minor scrapes.

I land on the wooden porch; broken shards of glass cutting into my hands and knees. With the weight of my fall, my cuts are much deeper than what was left in the pane of glass. Hot pain pulses along my knees and palms, but it's nothing compared to what would happen to me if I stayed in that house.

Getting to my feet, I have every intention of running as far as I have to in order to get the hell away from Carter and get help. But I don't get very far, stopping short as I hit a wall of muscle.

Tears spill over my eyes as I swing my fists, sure that it's one of his goons, but when I look up, I find the only person in the world I trust.

Mikhail Ivanov.

He wraps me in his arms, and I inhale his scent and the feeling of being with him once again. *Safe.* We hold each other for only a moment before Mikhail shoves me behind his back.

Carter opens the front door, but he stops short when he sees I have company. The excited smile slips off his face, and rage replaces it. He reaches into his back pocket, and I guess I'm still underestimating him because I do not expect the gun he pulls on us. My eyes go wide as saucers. Did he have that the whole time? This is so much worse than I feared.

He raises the gun, his eyes mean, and I fear my life is about to end or I'm about to watch Mikhail's death. I don't want my last moment on this earth facing Carter, so I turn to Mikhail, but he's not beside me. I shout his name as he runs at Carter. I distract the one with the gun, but not the determined director who owns my soul. He's quicker than the older man, and maybe Carter wasn't as ready to shoot as he seemed.

They grapple for the gun, and a shot fires. I shriek, but as far as I can tell, no one is injured. They continue to fight for another minute until there's another pop, and the tension between them immediately dissolves. I know in my bones one of them is dead or minutes away from it.

"Mikhail!" I shout.

My bloody hands cover my mouth, and I remember how Mikhail's hands were filled with glass just a couple of weeks ago. This porch was where Mom took pictures of me before every school year started. It's where she got dressed up and handed candy to the neighborhood kids. Our wholesome memories are washed away by blood. It drips between the floorboards, forever changing our old home history.

In the blink of an eye, everything changes. Carter falls, face ashen, and bright blood drips down his cheek. Mikhail is left standing and holding the smoking gun.

CHAPTER 27
MIKHAIL
FINALE

THE BULLET SINKS into Carter's skull, and I wish I could pretend the graphic spray of violence disgusts or displeases me, but it just feels good to kill who would dare hurt Lyla. She is mine, and no one will ever harm her again.

Carter abducted her, kept her in this house, and she had to crawl through the window to get away. I know we won't have any problem proving this was self-defense since the man ran toward us with a gun. My lawyers will make sure I'm clean of this mess.

Though while I'm deciding what legally happens next, Lyla remains in the same place. I place the gun on the floor and go to her, my soul shredding into pieces as she holds me and tremors run through her body. I hold her against my chest, my hand over her head, feeling her soft hair between my fingers.

"Dead. He's, he's dead."

"Good riddance." I want to spit on the ground beside him, but I don't want her to think less of me. A low sob starts to build in her throat, and she falls apart in my arms.

I look at the body that used to be Carter Livingston and try to make sense of my own feelings. I just killed a man. I took a life, and that's nothing I've ever thought I would do, but the pill is surprisingly easy to swallow when I remember everything he's done.

This mess needs to be cleaned, and we'll need to speak to the police. I have a list in mind of all the names I need to call, but Lyla's safety comes first. She can't stay here for another second. I scoop her into my arms because it's clear she's beyond reason or walking, and I press her tearstained cheek against my chest as I carry her back to the waiting car.

I place her in the passenger seat and buckle the seat belt for her. She cries so hard that she seems almost unaware of what's happening. I walk around the car, take the driver's seat, and start the car. My tension ticks higher as I drive. This is the second time I've done it in years. The first was on the way to her.

My hands tighten on the wheel, and I consider how much more I should have made that bastard suffer. His death was too quick. Lyla mumbles the whole way, barely making sense, until we enter the city and something clicks.

"You're driving."

I nod.

I would do anything for this woman. I knew what I was going to do when I went to her childhood home. Carter was too far gone, and if I wanted Lyla back, things were going to get ugly. I couldn't involve my driver in something illegal. While I was born and raised in privilege, I know it's not everyone's story. So I took the car and went to find her, hoping a cop wouldn't stop me and ask for my expired driver's license.

I don't know if Lyla knows how hard it was for me to get here, but when I glance at her, her eyes shine as if she does.

"Thank you for coming for me, Mikhail."

"Always."

We pull up outside the building, and even though I think she can probably walk, I carry her inside. She stares up at the lights and decorations with a childlike wonder that makes me worried she's slipping into shock. I wouldn't blame her. Watching a man die isn't an easy thing. Let alone one you spent most of your life loving and viewing as a father.

We climb on the elevator, and I rub circles over her back, waiting impatiently to reach the top floors. The doors open into the foyer, and she shakes in my arms.

"Cold?"

She shakes her head.

Fuck, definitely in shock.

I carry her through the house, up the stairs, and all the way to my own bedroom. Heading straight to the bathroom, I set her on the little bench and start stripping off my clothes. She doesn't even check what I'm doing until I start on hers. Finally, she aims curious brown eyes at me but doesn't say anything. I peel her T-shirt off and brush her hair away from her face.

"You're not going to ask me about it?" she whispers.

I shake my head. "When you're ready."

She holds my hand and stands. I help her out of her pants and underwear. Once we're both naked, I lift her into my arms, and we go in the shower.

Warm water sprays over us at the perfect pressure. I take a sponge and wash her. The dried blood on her body breaks me little by little. She's my pretty doll, meant to be pushed, pampered, and fucked. Never this.

As I lather her stomach, a sob breaks free from her throat, and she shakes as she cries. I abandon everything and hold her.

"He touched me," she says.

The world stops turning, and I'm not sure how to kill a man twice, but I'll find a way.

Lyla shakes her head. "He rubbed his dick on me. He touched my knee with his hand, and then when I was trying to get away, his face was in my ass. I hated it, and, and—"

"It's okay. It's over."

"I feel so dirty."

"You're not. Look at me. You're not."

"He wanted me to kiss him."

"You're only ever kissing me."

She reaches for me like the words are a great relief. Her hands lace around my neck, and I tip my head low, letting her take her time. Lyla goes on her tiptoes and kisses me.

"My body only belongs to you." She almost says it like a threat, as if I would disagree. I'll take pleasure in killing every man who tries to take her from me. She's mine and has always been.

Her kisses turn hungry. She bites my neck and whispers into my ear, "Show me I'm yours."

"If you don't know that you're mine yet, you're a worse student than I thought."

Lyla giggles, and my obsession with her grows. She seems like she might be nearly as crazy about me as I am about her. That's a red flag.

I grip her wet hair, narrowing my eyes.

"Turn around, and I'll show you who you belong to."

Her lips part, hungry for me, and she turns around. Her hands hold the tiles and give me the perfect view of her ass and pussy lips. Carving my fingers into her ass, I want to thoroughly mark her as mine.

I push two fingers into her pussy, a hiss slipping between my teeth when I realize how fucking wet she is. Her pussy grips my fingers like a vise, and my eyes roll back. I don't bother working her up because she doesn't need it. I trade my fingers for my cock, and the hot wet slide of her cunt nearly takes me out. I was so fucking worried about her.

Lyla cries my name, and I tip her head back with my fist, gripping her hair at the base of her neck. She's forced to look into my eyes as I pull her hair. I'm the one fucking this tight cunt. I'm the one she belongs to. The water falls between us, washing the past away.

That's enough of everyone else. Carter, this town, and the gossip. There's only Lyla and me now. My ballerina whore and I. My palm falls against her ass in a smack that echoes around the bathroom. She whimpers, her pussy getting even tighter. Encouraged by her response, I do it again, much harder, enjoying the sting in my palm as she whines and jumps at the contact. One more smack and her pussy comes around my cock, milking me so good.

She looks over her shoulder with a wicked smile I will never forget. "Mark me and make me come again."

Fuck.

"Jesus fucking Christ, Lyla. You greedy little whore."

This fucking woman. I slap her once again, the marks from my fingers painting her skin. I could come inside her, but I decide I'd rather make a splash. I pull out, and with a couple of strokes, I come all over her back and ass.

She's mine, now and forever.

CHAPTER 28
LYLA
FINALE

"ARE YOU READY, LYLA?" Maeve stands beside me, bouncing in excitement. To her, the adjustment to our cast is nothing but good news. I get the part she believes I always deserved, and she moves up to a better position than the one she had. "God, I'm so excited. It's our last show of the season. It's going to be good."

"It is," I agree.

"Why are you being so coy about it? Did our super-hot director already tell you what you're starring in for the spring production?" she asks with a salacious taunt.

"As a matter of fact, he has not." I spare that question only a scrap of my attention as the matter of my debut as Mikhail's prima ballerina is only a few short minutes away.

"Places, ladies!" Eduard calls, giving us a series of rapid claps to urge us on our way.

We take our places in the wings. Everyone is silent as the lights and music change. Mikhail's composition cues, and I remind myself I am the star of this show.

I am his. *Finally*.

Other dancers enter ahead of me, setting the stage and telling the story of the girl who wandered too far away in her search for berries to feed her sick and ailing family. She wandered into another world instead, one of fantastic and horrible things.

My cue comes, and I take the stage with a swirl of movement and fabric. My choreography is fast, frantic, and aching as I try to find medicine for my family. It slows as I approach the spot where I enter that other world, the magic confusing my senses. My steps are slow, dramatized, and clumsy.

I fall.

The audience gasps at the illusion, but I'm caught by a male dancer and set right, ready for my costume change and to get in position for the next dance.

The production moves smoothly, and the reality of being center stage again is so good it sings in every part of me. The only way it could possibly be better is if my mother was with me now. If only she could see me.

Mikhail took care of what happened with Carter. He never told me the details, but his lawyers came around one day, and the police took our statements. Besides that, he shielded me from the whole ordeal. Even the house is being taken care of, so it's out of my hands.

I'm glad Mom wasn't here to see the man he actually was. She never would have married Carter if she had known the monster she was bringing into our lives. I use the strange pain of his death to fuel the drama of my moves. Wedge that sadness and sense of triumph into my features as Mikhail's production shines.

I always knew we make art out of sadness. This ballet is about Mikhail's trauma, but I find a way to express mine too. This way, I turn something ugly into something beautiful with a twirl of my pointe.

The music reaches its final ascension, and my heart follows its beating, performing the last movements of this production. I end with my hands up in fifth position, and for a second too long, all I see is the blinding light shining on my face and the noise of my own breathing.

The moment ends, the audience claps, and the light lowers until I can see they are all standing. Tears run down my cheeks when I bow, humbled and grateful I'm here once again. I'm still standing after everything that happened, and more than that, I won. I'm back at the top.

When the curtain falls, I do too. Maeve kneels beside me, grabbing my hand and laughing. I forgot what it meant to be this joyful, not to feel like every step I take is heavy.

"It was amazing. You were amazing, Lyla!"

"You did great too," I tell her as we help one another up. "And now we are both members of this company. I expect donuts every morning."

She giggles. "The snacks are totally my responsibility, don't worry."

Mikhail waits for me right off the stage. His eyes shine and follow me everywhere I go like no one else is here. He hands me my jacket and my shoes.

"I need to change my clothes!" I say, but I take my pointe, using him to hold myself up and change to my Chucks.

"Not tonight." He comes closer to my ear. "I want to fuck you just like that."

I smile, my cheeks warming even though I know no one heard him. I put the jacket over my shoulders before following him outside. We leave through the front door, following the flux of people at the steps in front of the theater.

Mikhail gets impatient when people stop me to congratulate me. I know he's ready to have me to himself. He's greedy for my undivided attention. Tired of waiting, he tugs my arm, bringing me away from everyone and to the side of the steps.

"What's going on with you today?" I ask, sensing there's something beyond his normal silent brooding.

He stares, saying nothing until I feel entirely naked. I arch an eyebrow because I know he loves when I'm just as wicked as him. He gives me a slow kiss first. I hum in satisfaction, murmuring his name against his mouth.

"You were perfect today," he whispers between my lips.

Before I have a chance to react, he puts a small box between my hands with a note right on top.

> *Your body is epic poetry*
> *Your heart is a hungry flame*
> *I breathe for you*
> *-M.*

If that's not an I love you, I don't know what is. That's what I believe until I open the box and find my mother's necklace, the one Carter kept from me, and I decide, that no, this is the truest I love you I've ever seen.

EPILOGUE
LYLA

FIVE YEARS LATER

CHRISTMAS DAY.

It's my first thought when my eyes open. I reach for Mikhail, assuming he's asleep on his side of the bed, but of course he's not here anymore. That man wakes up too early.

I race downstairs, skipping as I go, and it's not only because this is my favorite time of the year. Mikhail is the better gift giver between us, and I'm so excited to see what he got me. It's funny because he always acts so tough, but he's thoughtful and observant. Of course he nails it every year.

But this year, I have a surprise, and he won't see it coming.

"Mikhail!" I yell, making a big fuss.

I find him in his office, his nose buried in paperwork. He has another production coming up this spring, and he's been stressed.

"No work today," I say, crossing my arms over my chest.

"Don't retire, and I can relax," he signs to me.

The signing took time and convincing, but eventually, he realized we needed a way of communicating that wasn't constantly hurting him. For more than fifteen years, he closed himself off from the world and was content not being heard often. But since I came into his life, there are a lot of things worth giving an opinion about.

"I think you'll survive with a new prima ballerina. And I'll be around anyway. It's not like I won't dance anymore."

He shoots me a look. As usual, it has the opposite effect, and I bite back a giggle. He's been complaining about my retirement announcement since I started playing with the idea. He likes that I'll be around more—no more long rehearsals and all that—but as a producer, he's been impossible, acting like it's the worst thing in the world to find someone to replace me.

I go to him, grab his hand in mine, and tug him away from his work. He's not going to find a new prima ballerina looking at paperwork on Christmas Day. I might like to be annoyed with how hard he works, or how hard I have to work to get his focus, but he's just being *Mikhail*, I guess.

"Come on. It's time for presents."

Mikhail drags his feet but follows me to the living room, where our tree sits. It's a perfect winter wonderland finally matching the outside of his iconic building. Before he has a chance to take a present from under the tree, I jump into action and take the one I have for him.

"I go first!"

I'm jumping up and down like a child. I've never been this excited before. He notices my nervous energy and narrows his eyes in suspicion, but I thrust the small box into his hands and nudge him to open it.

I bite my lip and hold my breath as he opens the narrow red box and finds his gift sitting there. He looks down and then back at me.

"This is serious?" he says so low I almost miss it.

"It is."

Mikhail takes the positive pregnancy test out of the box, looking at it as if it could be a trick, but it's right there in bold letters. I'm six weeks pregnant. I'm bouncing on the heels of my feet, and I don't see him coming when he takes me into his arms.

"My Lyla," he whispers into my ear, his arms around me and his nose buried in my hair.

I laugh. I planned this so carefully so we could have the perfect Christmas memory. And we'll have many of them now.

"I guess I'm okay if you retire. Having you barefoot and pregnant could be very interesting," he signs to me.

"No pointe with my belly?"

"Definitely not. I think you'll find I'm even more overbearingly protective now."

"I think I can live with that."

"I wouldn't be so sure."

I squeal and giggle as he scoops me into his arms, and minutes later, we're under the Christmas tree enjoying the best present of all—us.

Looking for a darker and crazier Christmas retelling? Sacked and Sleighed

ALSO BY THE AUTHORS

Need another holiday novella, but darker and crazier?
Sacked and Sleighed by Aurelia Knight

Looking for a little sweet and cozy, but dirty Christmas?

Looking for more Ballerina's and fallen heroes?
Bond to Break

Want to read Maeve's story? Stay tuned for details on "Dare me Daisy"

ABOUT THE AUTHORS

Aurelia and Amy met by chance and have become fast friends since. Blending their styles of dark and emotional, they bring you stories that will stick with you and leave you questioning.

ACKNOWLEDGMENTS

Amy and Aurelia would like to thank their friends and service professionals that helped bring this book to life. There are too many of you to name, but you are each so special to us.

Editing by Jenny Simms with Editing4Indies
Original Cover Design by Kirsty Still with Pretty Little Design Co.
Art Cover Portrait by Oksana Bersan
Formatting and Interior by Aurelia Knight

Milton Keynes UK
Ingram Content Group UK Ltd.
UKHW031159061224
452240UK00001B/34